against him

Christian missed a step.

She tried to pull away.

He wouldn't let her.

His hand moved over her back, circling.

Sonya trembled.

His lips moved to her jawline, to her ear.

Sonya turned her mouth toward his. Their lips met, touched, pulled away, met again, parted.

His eyes glittered when he met her look....

Nothing like this had ever happened before. Christian Townsend was like a drug to her system. The more she was with him, the more she *wanted* to be with him. And the more she wanted to be with him, the more she wanted. Sonya shivered even in the heat of her embarrassment. What was she going to do?

ABOUT THE AUTHOR

Ginger Chambers gets story ideas from a variety
of sources. Sometimes she starts with a specific
character in mind, puts the person in a situation
and watches as the action starts to evolve.

A native of Texas, Ginger has returned with her
husband and their two children to live in her home
state after having resided in California for a
number of years.

Books by Ginger Chambers
HARLEQUIN AMERICAN ROMANCE

 32–GAME OF HEARTS
 71–PASSION'S PREY
107–IN LOVE'S SHADOW
169–WHEN HEARTS COLLIDE
238–FIREFLY IN THE NIGHT
254–CALL MY NAME SOFTLY
288–PASSAGES OF GOLD

Don't miss any of our special offers. Write to us at the
following address for information on our newest releases.

Harlequin Reader Service
901 Fuhrmann Blvd., P.O. Box 1397, Buffalo, NY 14240
Canadian address: P.O. Box 603,
Fort Erie, Ont. L2A 5X3

NIGHTSHADE

GINGER CHAMBERS

Harlequin Books

TORONTO • NEW YORK • LONDON
AMSTERDAM • PARIS • SYDNEY • HAMBURG
STOCKHOLM • ATHENS • TOKYO • MILAN

For my mother
Annie Christine Pregeant Smith
1907-1989
"If only love could make things right."

Published March 1990

First printing January 1990

ISBN 0-373-16335-5

Copyright © 1990 by Ginger Chambers. All rights reserved.
Except for use in any review, the reproduction or utilization
of this work in whole or in part in any form by any electronic,
mechanical or other means, now known or hereafter invented,
including xerography, photocopying and recording,
or in any information storage or retrieval system, is forbidden without
the permission of the publisher, Harlequin Enterprises Limited,
225 Duncan Mill Road, Don Mills, Ontario, Canada M3B 3K9.

All the characters in this book have no existence outside the
imagination of the author and have no relation whatsoever to
anyone bearing the same name or names. They are not even
distantly inspired by any individual known or unknown to the
author, and all incidents are pure invention.

® are Trademarks registered in the United States Patent and
Trademark Office and in other countries.

Printed in U.S.A.

Prologue

The tiny glass bottle caught a ray of the sun, causing emerald fire to light the features of the small boy holding it. Fascinated, he twisted it around, trying to make the light reappear. But no matter how hard he tried, the flash of green would not recur.

The boy turned to some of the other objects spread out on the table before him—a comb with dancing figures carved along its ivory spine, a drinking cup, a whimsically painted fan. But the bottle beckoned him once again.

It had been the first object to draw his attention after the long flight he made alone from New York to Italy, and he already knew some of its history. His great-uncle had told him that the bottle was old, very old, and at one time it had held the taste of death.

He ran a finger across the delicately formed leaf that was embossed on the rounded surface. It looked so real that it might have been a living leaf transformed into glass by the touch of a magician. Poisonous po-

tions and magicians almost always mixed. Why, in one
of his favorite books there was a magician who—

Hands came to rest on his thin shoulders, bringing
him back to the rich aroma of his great-uncle's favorite cigar. "So, my little Christian, you like my collection. I thought you might."

The boy turned around, his dark curling hair falling over his forehead, his blue eyes inquisitive. "You
found all of this yourself, Uncle?"

The old man nodded. He was tall and spare and
impeccably groomed, with an air of past adventure.
His midnight-blue eyes, so similar in color to his great-
nephew's, were permanently marked at the corners
with an array of wrinkles. His skin, burned brown by
an unrelenting sun, had long since lost the unhealthy
pallor of his own childhood. He nodded again, smiling.

The boy held out the bottle. "I like this one best!"

His uncle took the object and unconsciously mim-
icked the boy's earlier action of holding it to the sun.
"Why do you say that?"

The boy shrugged. "I don't know."

His uncle chuckled. He understood the compelling
lure of danger even if the boy did not. "Look no farther than your own blood, my Christian. With pirates
for ancestors, you've inherited a knack for balancing
on the sharp edge of the sword. But be careful, one
wrong step...one wrong move, and...".

Christian giggled. "And there would be *two* of
me!"

The old man gazed down at the laughing face. Even in a child as young as six, the Townsend characteristics showed strongly. He saw the familiar recklessness, the challenge given and accepted, the sheer joy of life that was made all the sweeter by the knowledge that it could disappear within the blink of an eye. He also saw the charm that made it all worthwhile. For a moment he experienced a pang of jealousy. His life was ending as Christian's was beginning. He wanted to do it all over again! But, continuing to look into the childish face, he knew that Christian deserved his time, his moments of glory in a world crammed with opportunity.

He ruffled the child's hair. "Not two," he corrected. "Only one. One that might not be so easily put together again. Take care, my Christian. Always remember to step cautiously, even when boldness is needed to achieve an end."

The boy's smile faded, and for a moment he looked far older than his years. "I will, Uncle," he promised. Then, like quicksilver, his smile returned. "Now tell me about the bottle...about how you found it...and about what used to be inside."

The old man was pleased. All he had left were his memories and his stories. Yet he had so many of them, and now, for the short few weeks of summer, he had a child who would not tire of hearing them.

He sat down in a wide chair in a shaded area of the courtyard and patted the cushion at his side, an action that instantly caused Christian to abandon the table.

"Now, let me think—" he mused softly as the boy wiggled into position beside him.

The warm Italian sun spread its golden light over the surrounding hills; a light breeze touched their skin, refreshing them. In the distance, a bird cried for its mate.

As he waited for his uncle's tale to unfold, Christian clutched the emerald bottle to his chest.

Chapter One

Sonya Douglas hurried through the cavernous hall, her footsteps echoing as she moved from one area of the deserted museum to the next. She didn't pause as she came to a heavy door, pushed against it and descended a flight of stairs to the open rooms below that were her realm.

Voices guided her past the padded work tables where she and her assistants labored and beyond the rows of open shelving where articles not presently exhibited were stored. When she came into view, David Pewter, the museum's curator of European art, broke away from his companion to meet her.

A worried frown darkened his brow. "You're here. I was beginning to wonder!"

"I came as quickly as I could. What's happened? Has there been a leak?" Sonya glanced at the floor. Workmen had been renovating the museum's ancient plumbing system for the past three weeks. A water leak could be catastrophic.

David shook his head.

"What is it then?" she asked.

Instead of answering, he drew her toward a gaping hole in the nearest interior wall and handed her a flashlight. "Look inside," he said.

Sonya stared at him. "I don't understand."

"Just *look*," he repeated.

Since David was normally a quiet, unassuming person, uncomfortable with giving orders, Sonya did as he requested. Fine particles of dust floated in the air and she was about to shield her nose when she spotted a length of white sheeting crumpled on the rough interior floor. Peering closer, she saw what looked to be museum artifacts spilling out of it. "What's that doing there?" she asked, drawing back, surprised. She had forgotten all about her threatened sneeze.

"I have no idea," David said.

"Is this some kind of joke?"

"Not that I know of. A workman was opening the wall to get to a section of pipe. When he saw the sheeting, he pulled on it, and what you saw came rolling out. The workman told his foreman, who called security—" he indicated his uniformed companion "—who called me. I hadn't gone home yet. Then I called you."

"I still don't understand. Who'd put . . . ?"

David shrugged.

Sonya leaned back into the hole and steadied the beam of light upon the objects. A drinking cup, a serving dish, a comb and a small green bottle were revealed. She straightened. "Do you think they could be part of a collection?"

"That's why I called you." David turned to the guard. "We can handle it from here, Wally. Thanks."

The security guard tipped his hat before departing. Sonya barely noticed his action, her mind playing with her previous question. "Because if they are—"

"All hell is going to break loose. I know. That's what I'm afraid of."

Sonya was silent. Finally, she took a deep breath. "Well, we can't just leave them there."

"Even though I did think about it."

"David!"

"Well, I did, I'll be honest. With everything that's been happening around here lately, we don't need another complication."

"But we can't do that!"

David rubbed the back of his neck. "I know. I know."

"Anyway, they may not be anything important. Just some things someone overlooked."

"Inside a wall ... sure."

"There's only one way to find out."

UNDER THE STRONG LIGHT of her work lamp, Sonya examined the drinking cup. As registrar, she was in charge of logging each article that entered or left the museum, as well as inspecting and noting its condition. Any object that had been housed in either this museum or any other would have an identification number somewhere on its surface. On this particular cup, the number was etched beneath its base.

"It's not ours," she murmured. "The numbers are a different pattern."

"Then it's something on loan. I'm beginning to have a bad feeling about this."

Sonya extended the cup. "What period would you say?"

David examined it. "Try Renaissance Florence."

From rather modest beginnings, the practice of museum record-keeping had evolved into a rather complicated procedure. Each painting or article was filed and cross-filed, each record meticulously kept. Of art works on exhibition or in storage, a current roster was maintained. Records reaching back into the distant past, though, were usually incomplete. And considering that this particular museum dated back into the previous century, the task that lay ahead could have been daunting. Sonya's only salvation was that the previous registrar had done her best to organize the museum's older records as her way of contributing to the institution's history. She had even cross-referenced her system. If David said the cup was from Renaissance Florence, a record most likely would be found.

Sonya consulted the proper file in the inactive catalogue, her fingers flipping through the three by five cards that were labeled by number in the Renaissance Florence—Household Utensils index.

Then her fingers stopped and a startled breath was jerked into her lungs.

David saw her reaction and pushed her to one side, replacing her frozen fingers with his own. Soon he was echoing the same quick intake of breath. His gaze flew to hers. "The Townsend exhibit!" he rasped.

"What are we going to do?" she asked.

The situation had been bad enough earlier when they thought that what they had found might be simply a misplaced exhibit. But this! This had the capacity not merely to rock the museum's already shaky foundation . . . but to destroy it!

"Hang ourselves?" David suggested.

TED ARMSTRONG, THE MUSEUM'S assistant director, stormed into the registration area. "This had better be good!" he growled. "I was having dinner with one of the board of trustees. Do you *know* what it looked like for me to have to rush away like that? God's teeth! The last thing we need is to give rise to any more questions!"

"We wouldn't have disturbed you if it wasn't important," David said.

The assistant director's fiery gaze settled on the curator. "What is it then? Come on . . . tell me."

Sonya drew his attention, motioning toward the objects—eight in all—that had been found outside and inside the sheeting. "These were discovered by a workman. We think—" She amended, "We *know* it's the Townsend exhibit." While waiting for his arrival, she had searched out the original exhibition list that described each piece and confirmed the identity of the full collection.

Ted Armstrong was perfectly still. "What stupid— What are you talking about?" He didn't believe her.

"It's the missing exhibit," she repeated.

Ted snatched the list from her hand and repeated the confirmation process she had followed previously. Finally, groping for a chair, he wheezed weakly, "My God!"

"They were hidden inside a wall. That one over there," David explained.

The assistant director followed his gesture, but he was having so much trouble comprehending the reality of the moment that he merely blinked at the devastated wall.

Sonya fingered the edge of the table and David shifted from foot to foot as they waited for the assistant director to recover. The wait was not long. Ted jerked to his feet and demanded, "Who else knows about this?"

"Just us," David said.

"What about the workman? What's his name?"

"I'm not sure. Wally can tell us."

"Wally knows, too?"

"He was notified when the discovery was made. So was the plumber's foreman. But none of them have any idea about what..."

Ted interrupted, "We have to keep this quiet! If someone from the media were to catch wind of this, it could be the final blow for both Dr. Hockly *and* the museum."

Sonya and David exchanged quick glances. Julian Hockly had been the museum's director for the past five years and was admired by each of his employees. It was considered purely bad luck that his stewardship had seen so much trouble. No one thought he deserved it.

"What can we do?" Sonya asked.

Ted turned his hard gaze on her. "First, don't say anything to anyone...and I do mean *anyone*. Not the slightest hint that something unusual has happened here. Next, since we're the only ones to know about this, it's up to us to resolve it."

David questioned, "You *are* going to tell Dr. Hockly, aren't you?"

"Of course." The assurance was curt.

"And the insurance company," Sonya said. "They'll have to know. Things could get pretty sticky if we don't tell them."

"Yes . . . yes." Ted began to pace.

"And the owner," Sonya added, knowing that she was compounding Ted's list of difficulties. But if anyone had the right to learn of the discovery, it was the owner.

"God almighty!" he exploded. "Why don't we just take out a front-page ad?"

David withdrew into himself. Normally when the assistant director raged, he made sure to be elsewhere. But this time there was nowhere else for him to go.

Sonya reverted to fingering the edge of the table. She had never been a particular fan of Ted Armstrong. She felt that the man enjoyed his temperamental outbursts a little too much. But, at the moment, she could understand his frustrations.

The assistant director ran a hand through his iron-gray hair. "For the time being," he decided, "we'll leave things as they are. I'll talk with Dr. Hockly...see what he suggests." He glanced at the objects on the table as if he wished they had never been found. "Sonya, put those...things...someplace where no one will stumble on to them. David, you come with me. I want some kind of backup when I talk to Dr. Hockly."

David got quickly to his feet, but before leaving the room he directed a baleful glance toward Sonya. To bolster his resolve, she gave him a quick thumbs-up sign, but without any confidence.

ALONE NOW, SONYA SLID into her chair. Even beneath the light's harsh glow, the collection appeared to have little merit. It was really rather ordinary. None of the pieces were made from gold or silver or listed as being fashioned by a famous artisan. Its disappearance thirty years before should never have warranted such a storm of controversy, nor should the scandal have reached such a peak. The collection was interesting, but not nearly as valuable as the majority of others the museum housed...either then or now. Only the fact that it *had* disappeared set it apart.

As she continued to stare at the objects, a flash of green fire suddenly sparked against the light, reflecting against her face, lighting her small section of the room.

Startled, Sonya sat back. Had it been real? As a test, she wiggled the table, hoping for another display. But this time there was no spark, no fire. The green bottle—it had to have been the green bottle—remained muted.

Sonya released a pent-up breath. This was the end of a very long day, one she had thought to have finished hours before. It was also the beginning of a great deal more. The Townsend collection might be ordinary, but its rediscovery and the repercussions that could follow were like charged particles from a nuclear cloud—anything *but* ordinary.

She could be excused for experiencing one small hallucination.

Chapter Two

"Hildie, wake up! If you don't get moving soon, you'll be late!"

The admonishment did little good. Ten minutes later Sonya was back at her younger sister's door, repeating an abbreviated version of the words. Finally, a groggy reply signaled some success.

As she hurried downstairs for a quick breakfast, Sonya shook her head. Sometimes she wondered how she and Hildie managed. Their personalities were so different. Where she greeted each morning with a modicum of welcome, Hildie would much rather not start the day until noon. Where she was practical, her sister was impetuous. Where she hummed along on a smooth, even keel, everything in Hildie's life was either absolutely wonderful or absolutely awful. Perhaps it was her sister's age—eighteen was not an easy time—but Sonya didn't remember having gone through such an upheaval. Of course, that had been at the time of their parents' divorce and life had had enough ups and downs without any outside help from her. Not to mention that she'd had the eight-year-old

Hildie to care for, as well as their father until he died.
It was a good thing she *was* of a steady frame of mind.

Sonya's stomach lurched. Steady. Right now she
didn't feel the least bit steady, not when she remembered what she would have to face at the museum that
morning. Last night, while putting the Townsend
pieces in an out-of-the-way drawer, she had felt as if
she were handling nitroglycerin. And that feeling was
not going to improve.

"What's the matter? Why are you looking so
grim?"

Sonya looked up to see Hildie clumping downstairs
while attempting to suppress a yawn. Even with her
chestnut hair tousled and her bathrobe hanging loosely
over a rumpled gown, Hildie's natural prettiness was
not dimmed.

"I was just remembering...I have some extra things
to do at the museum that will keep me late today."

"So you want me to make dinner?"

"If you wouldn't mind. I'll warm mine up when I
get in."

"Sure. No problem."

Sonya rinsed her cup and plate and gave an esti-
mating glance at her watch before giving the same es-
timating look at her sister. "Now you're not going to
go back to sleep when I leave, are you?"

A smile tilted Hildie's lips as she sat down at the
table. "I can't make any promises."

"Well, try not to, okay? This isn't high school. The
Institute's waiting list is at least a mile long."

Hildie's smile changed to an expression of moody
contemplation. "I'm not sure if I should keep doing

this, Sonya. I don't think I'm talented enough. I'm just taking up the space of someone else who'd do so much better."

"Those fabric designs you showed me last week were beautiful!"

Hildie shrugged. "Beginner's luck."

"Oh, Hildie, no! That's not true. Why, if I tried to do one...well, you've heard of a monkey trying to oil paint?"

Hildie giggled.

Sonya smiled encouragement. "Promise you'll give it a little longer and not make any rash decisions, not without really thinking it through?"

Hildie's brown gaze met the equally brown gaze of her sister. Behind the earnest request, she saw the fierce determination that had kept them a family unit when otherwise they might have been torn apart. "Okay," she agreed. "I'll stick with it for a little while longer...for you."

Sonya squeezed her sister's shoulder. "You won't regret it. Now don't forget, I'll probably be late."

"I won't."

As she leaned forward to kiss the smooth cheek, Hildie stifled another yawn.

THE YOUTHFUL GIGGLE that followed their botched attempt at a loving parting rang lightly in Sonya's ears as she hurried down the tall steps that fronted the old Victorian she and Hildie rented half of on the outskirts of the city. The other tenant, an elderly man who had retired some years before from the San Francisco Fire Department, greeted her as he retrieved his

morning newspaper. Normally, she enjoyed stopping
to converse with their neighbor, Mr. O'Dwyer, but
today she escaped after a quick exchange of pleasant-
ries, leaving him standing on the steps grumbling
about one of the day's headlines.

Even then she barely managed to catch her bus and
after another quick glance at her watch, settled into
her seat and tried to relax. But soon her mind began
to skip back and forth from her difficulties with Hildie to the difficulties of her job. She didn't know
which problem was most perplexing.

If only there was a way to make Hildie see how
much she had to offer the world. She was smart,
capable and definitely talented. But whenever told
those things, Hildie discounted them as words a loving sister felt compelled to say, and therefore not to be
believed. One day Hildie would learn the truth, but
until that time Sonya had a battle on her hands trying
not to let her sister sell herself short.

Her other battle involved the museum. If anyone
thought employment at such a place was dull, that
person was crazy. Particularly at this museum, where
they seemed to rocket from one crisis to the next. Over
the past six months they had been accused of know-
ingly exhibiting forgeries, of carelessly handling stored
objects and of more than one financial irresponsibil-
ity. That on top of several previous accusations had
left the museum teetering on the brink. Even though
none of the rumors and accusations were true, each
time one surfaced, damage was done. A museum ex-
isted on trust, and trust, for them, was wearing dan-

gerously thin. Now, with the reappearance of the Townsend exhibit, something that was actually true...

Even years ago, halfway across the country where their father had been curator of sculpture in a Houston museum, reverberations from the scandal had echoed loudly through the corps. Growing up and hearing about it as a child, Sonya had never dreamed that one day she would be working in the museum where the incident took place. Neither had she dreamed that she would be a participant in its return.

When she had told Hildie that she would be late this evening, it was no empty promise. The lost articles would have to be checked carefully for damage and compared with the original exhibition statement. New notations would have to be made as to their current condition. And none of that could be done while her assistants were in the registration area. She would have to wait until everyone else left.

As she thought of all the obstacles that lay ahead, she groaned in dismay, which caused the woman sitting next to her to dart her a suspicious look.

Covering her unwitting slip, Sonya forced a weak smile and lightly pressed a hand to her midsection, pretending to have an upset stomach. At the next stop, the woman got off. Whether it was her original intent or a quick escape, Sonya didn't know.

The seat was soon reclaimed, and Sonya made sure to keep any further show of emotion strictly to herself. No use upsetting another person.

Still, an amused smile broke through and the features that each morning she considered to be merely

comfortable in comparison to Hildie's were blessed
with a sylphlike attraction all their own.

SONYA WAS HALFWAY UP the long series of steps leading to the museum's rear entrance when a hailing call
caught her attention.

"Hello— Please wait!"

As she turned, she was ready with a smile, expecting a friend, but as soon as she recognized the slightly
overweight, middle-aged woman hurrying toward her,
her smile disappeared and her next instinct was to
sprint the rest of the distance to the door and barri-
cade herself inside.

In reality, she did swing away, her body poised for
flight, but the woman was too quick. She was beside
her before Sonya could complete her first step toward
escape.

"Oh, my! That was...quite...a run," the reporter puffed.

Sonya again started to pull away, but the woman's
hand shot out to stop her.

"No, I'm fine. Just...give me a second...to catch
my breath."

"I'm late," Sonya replied tersely. "I don't have
time."

There was an immediate recovery. "What's this I
hear about something exciting happening at the
museum? Something *very* exciting."

Ice crystals formed in Sonya's bloodstream. *How
had the woman found out?* It was all she could do not
to let her panic show. "I don't know what you're
talking about," she denied.

The woman laughed. "Oh, come now. Do you really expect me to believe that?"

"I still don't know what you're talking about."

Avaricious blue eyes bored into her, probing deeply for a crack, until, at last, the pressure on Sonya's arm lessened and she was able to withdraw it.

"No, I don't suppose you do. And even if you did, you'd die before telling me anything, wouldn't you?"

"I'm late," Sonya repeated tonelessly.

"I've never been early for anything in my life, except a story. And I smell a story. Right here...right now!"

"It's probably the smog."

The woman gave another grating laugh. "San Francisco doesn't have any smog, remember? At least, that's what the city fathers want us to print so that all the tourists will come here and spend their money." Her eyes again slid over Sonya's uncompromising stance before she finally said with sarcastic spite, "Oh, go on! Don't let me keep you. I wouldn't *dream* of getting you into trouble."

Sonya walked away with a stiffly held back.

She didn't follow the usual route to her work area. Instead, she chose a familiar path to another office and after giving a sharp rap on the door, let herself inside.

David half rose at her precipitous entry.

"Do you know who I just met outside?" she demanded.

"Who?"

"Millicent Walker."

David sank slowly back into his chair. "What did she want?"

"She asked me if anything 'exciting' had happened at the museum recently. Anything *very* exciting."

David paled. "Do you think she knows?"

Sonya paused to consider the question. Now that she had expressed her anger and fear, she began to see the situation more clearly. "She'd like us to think so," she answered carefully, "but if she does know, why would she try to get information out of me? Why wouldn't she go straight to the top...or straight to that sleazy newspaper of hers? Print first and ask questions later, isn't that their motto?"

"She's little more than a gossip columnist!"

"She used to be one. Someone told me that."

"It fits." David snorted. "That rag she works for is no better than a tabloid. It's definitely not one of San Francisco's more responsible papers. But people seem to love to read it."

Sonya slid into a spare chair. "She almost scared the life out of me, I can tell you that."

"She could scare a grizzly bear!"

The two of them were laughing when Ted Armstrong slammed into the room without knocking.

"All right! Who did it? Which one of you talked?" His bullish gaze sliced into them. "I've just been accosted by that female shark who calls herself a reporter. She says she knows something." His fist crashed down on David's desk, making the younger man jump. "There're only a few people it could be. And it sure as hell isn't me!"

"Did you talk to her?" Sonya asked. "I mean...did you let her know that we'd found something?"

"Hell, no! I told her she was crazy!"

Great public relations, Sonya thought dryly.

"She seems to think she's on to something," Ted continued, "and we all know there's only one thing that could be. It couldn't have been either of the workmen because I had a special talk with them. They know that to say *anything* about what goes on in this museum is enough to get them blackballed from this town forever. And it wasn't Wally—that man can keep a secret from his own unconscious. So, who did it? Which one of you opened your mouth and threw the museum down the drain? Which of you is so ungrateful that you'd..."

Sonya pushed stiffly to her feet and walked to within half an inch of the assistant director's face. He stopped ranting once he saw the look in her usually quiet eyes. "Neither of us," she said tightly. "And if you'd stop shouting long enough to listen, we'd have saved you the trouble of wasting all that hot air.

"She accosted me, too, if you're interested. Pretended that she knew something. But I didn't say anything...either then or earlier. Neither did David. The woman's just trying to sniff out a story, Ted, trying to see if she can get one of us to react, and then she'd know she was on to something. So you'd better think back. Did you, by your reaction, give her cause to dig deeper?"

The assistant director was stunned by her attack and also shocked at the truth of her words. She could see in his eyes that he was concentrating, reliving his encounter with the reporter. She saw the doubt that he temporarily could not hide.

Sonya turned away, sickened by the confrontation. Deserving or not, she had berated her superior in front of another employee. She loved her job at the museum. She didn't want to leave it—or San Francisco.

She glanced at David, who was looking at her with stricken eyes. He knew what she might have brought on herself.

She cleared her throat. "I'm sorry. I didn't mean to snap at you like that. It's just that I'm on edge, like everyone else."

The assistant director's body was tense. Sonya watched as he forced himself to relax. When he spoke, his voice was flat. "Forget it. As you say, everyone is tense."

Sonya hadn't thought to get off so easily and gave a mental sigh. But Ted wasn't through with her yet.

"Dr. Hockly and I talked again this morning," he said. "He's left it to my discretion how we handle the situation. He's called the insurance company; a representative will be here later today. And he tried to place a call to the owner, but it seems that the man is dead. His nephew is coming in his place. Sonya," Ted shot her a glance that glimmered of revenge. "You can babysit the nephew. David, I want you to work with the insurance company. I'll do my part by talking with the police. I'm not sure exactly how the statute of limitations will work in this case. Hopefully in our favor. We certainly don't want to have detectives nosing around at the same time Millicent What's-her-name is sniffing the trail." He turned back to David.

"The insurance company has as much desire to keep this under wraps as we do, so you shouldn't have any trouble there."

"Sonya." Again the get-even glimmer. "The nephew is an unknown quantity. Keep him quiet . . . whatever it takes. He's your responsibility."

"But—" Sonya started to protest.

"You have a complaint?" Ted inquired silkily.

Sonya bit her lip. "No."

"He arrives tomorrow afternoon. Whatever you do, *don't* antagonize him with the sweetness of your personality."

She heard David's hiss of breath. Ted was revelling in being nasty to her in front of the witness to his own upbraidment.

To show that she might be bloodied but unbowed, Sonya lifted her chin as she accepted the challenge. "Of course."

The assistant director made no further comment before exiting the room.

To her later shame, Sonya couldn't resist the childish urge to poke out her tongue at Ted's departing back, causing David to snicker in appreciation.

Chapter Three

Christian Townsend adjusted his legs, trying once again for comfort. Even in the roomier first-class section, his long body became cramped if he were trapped in one position for too long. And the eleven-hour flight from London to San Francisco definitely could be defined as *trapped*. The lounge provided some relief, but only as a temporary escape.

A soft metallic *ping* sounded, another passenger making a demand. As the attendant hurried by, she smiled at Christian. More than a flicker of interest was evident in her eyes. On her way to the gallery, she paused to speak to him.

"Is there anything I can get for you? Coffee? A soft drink? Something stronger?"

Christian shook his head. "No, thanks."

"A magazine?"

Christian again shook his head. "I'm fine. How much longer until we land?"

She glanced at her watch, happy to have an excuse to linger. "About thirty minutes. We've been fighting a head wind, so we've had some time added. Captain Philips should be making the announcement soon.''

At that moment the pilot's voice sounded throughout the plane and the attendant's smile deepened when he repeated her exact words.

"Good timing," Christian murmured. "Think you could do it again?"

"We practice all the time."

Another metallic *ping* rang out a short distance away. The attendant glanced toward the passenger and nodded acknowledgement. Still, she didn't leave Christian's side. "Are you sure I can't do anything for you?" There was enough promise in her voice to give the question added meaning.

His midnight-blue eyes twinkled appreciatively before settling into regret. "Another time, possibly?"

Disappointment colored her smile. Recovering, she said, "If you change your mind, just press the button."

Amusement glimmered across Christian's handsome features as he watched her move toward the other passenger. The smooth curve of her hip, the nipped-in waist, the slender length of her legs might, under other circumstances, have been tempting. She also seemed to have the jaunty spirit he enjoyed, but this trip was not being made for pleasure. It claimed a much more serious nature from which he couldn't allow himself to be drawn.

He again tried for a measure of comfort, conscious of not disturbing his seatmate, who had been sleeping since halfway across the Atlantic. Christian envied the man his talent. He was never able to sleep on a commercial airliner himself. A part of his mind always insisted upon going over each technical adjustment with the pilot—a curse he understood others who were licensed to fly shared. It was hard to let someone else do the driving when that person had different methods and reflexes than yours.

He opened the paperback he had purchased at Heathrow but was still unable to get past the third chapter. With a sigh, he glanced out the window. From his aisle position, all he could see was distant cloud tops.

The whine of the jet's engines diminished slightly and soon the plane started to buffet as they crossed through turbulent air beginning their drawn-out descent. It reminded him of his first flight to San Francisco as a child, with his great-uncle. The reason for their journey, then, had been the exact opposite of the one calling him now: his uncle's favorite collection had disappeared mysteriously.

The jet bounced, hitting another pocket of unstable air, before steadying. To entertain his seven-year-old nephew, Uncle Dominic had told him stories about giants who hid among the clouds and played with the metal birds that invaded their world. In an echo of memory, Christian could hear his own childish laughter responding to the warm, rich voice of the man he had grown to love. "Giants, Uncle?" he had giggled.

That was the last time he had laughed so happily on that trip. His uncle had been heartbroken at the loss of his collection and had become so angry with the way the investigation was handled.

"I don't believe it, my little Christian! I don't believe for one second that it could happen the way these *imbeciles* are saying! Something is wrong. Someone is not telling the truth!"

When they had met with the museum's top official for the final time before returning to Italy, his uncle had demanded, "What reason do you have for believing the worst of this wretched man you say has stolen my collection? Why? Because he is poor? Because he is down on his luck? Me? I do not believe it! I have talked with him. He says he is innocent."

"But, Professor Townsend, everyone who is guilty claims to be innocent!"

Dominic drew to his full height, becoming a commanding presence. "What proof do you have? That he drives a truck? That he was taking a shipment of goods to the rail station...of which my collection was supposed to be a part? At this moment no one seems to know for sure! There are no papers, no directives. And why would my little collection be the only property stolen? It is truly valuable only to me."

"But Tomas Delia doesn't know that, sir! He's a stupid man...a desperate man."

"I believe him," Dominic answered.

"We will have the truth from him soon."

"The truth will remain hidden. You will find no words of enlightenment. Not from him." Placing a hand on Christian's shoulder, his uncle had said sadly, "Come, my Christian, we will go."

"As soon as we know anything, we'll contact you." The director remained determined.

Dominic didn't reply as they walked away.

Christian had felt so small beside his great-uncle, like a young soul wandering the corridors of time in the company of a much more ancient being who was suffering greatly.

For the rest of that summer—his second in the company of his uncle—their existence had been melancholy. His uncle had tried to dispel his sadness, but the grouping of artifacts had been so special to him. They had come from his very first archaeological discovery, when both he and the world were younger.

Not even the arrival of word that the driver had been released from jail due to a lack of evidence, confirming Dominic's instinctive knowledge, had cheered his uncle. The objects still remained lost to him. It was as if a part of his heart had gone missing, as well...

The seat-belt light flashed on for the final time and the attendants started down each aisle, checking to see that everyone was in compliance and that each seat was properly positioned for landing. Once more Christian received a special smile, but this time he barely recognized it.

Whenever he remembered the pain his uncle had endured, the irony of the collection's reappearance a short few weeks after his death twisted Christian's heart. It also firmed his resolve that this time the truth lurking behind all those many years of mourning would be served.

SONYA'S NERVES WERE tightly stretched as the day wore on. From her first step into the museum that morning, there had been one frustration after another and repeated calls had been made to straighten everything out. And all the while, she'd had a monstrous threat hanging over her head. What was she going to say to him? *Oh, sorry. We lost your family's prized collection, but it's turned up again. Here it is. Now go away. And, by the way, please don't tell anyone.* Somehow she didn't think that would suffice.

The telephone at her elbow rang and she jumped, instinct telling her that the moment she dreaded had arrived. She let it ring again before answering.

Julia Montgomery, at the front security desk, said, "Someone to see you, Sonya. A Mr. Townsend. Shall I send him on, or do you want to come get him?"

"I'll come," she decided quickly.

"Lucky you," was the murmured reply.

Sonya frowned. What in the world...?

CHRISTIAN SAUNTERED into the giftshop, a small open area that took up a portion of the museum to one side of the front doors. Inside was everything that an art aficionado could want as a souvenir: reproductions of paintings housed in the museum, books on the artifacts represented there, circulars on special showings and every conceivable knickknack from postcards of San Francisco to pencils with a picture of the museum emblazoned on their sides.

Christian was flicking through an array of keychains, fascinated by the many choices, when he became aware of someone at his side.

"Mr. Townsend?"

A woman's voice drew his attention. She was of medium height and carrying just the right amount of weight to round out her delicate frame properly. Her hair, the color of ripe wheat, drew a sharp contrast to eyes that were a warm, rich brown. Her nose was small and narrow above a mouth that at other times might be smiling but was now being held under tight control. She was more interesting looking than beautiful, with an ethereal quality that even at first glance could prove illusive.

Christian turned back to the key chains. He tapped the nearest, making them all rattle. "I would have thought this kind of thing would be more suitable in a tourist trap than a museum."

She ignored his remark. "I'm Sonya Douglas, senior registrar here. If you'd follow me, please."

Christian jangled the key chains once again before nodding.

"This way," Sonya said, aware that he was following her without turning. Now she understood Julie's murmured, "Lucky you." To anyone susceptible to physical good looks, the man behind her was outstanding: jet black hair curling loosely to his collar, dark blue eyes set off by long thick lashes, classical masculine features with the hint of a cleft in his chin, a long lean body that he carried with both power and ease. Though, considering the strain she was under, he could have been Michelangelo's *David* come to life and she would be too unsettled to care. This was the man she was going to have to deal with. The man she would have to hustle away as quickly as she could, in as quiet a manner as possible. No shadow of suspicion could be cast. Everything had to be handled carefully—and she wasn't totally sure that she could do it.

After closing the door to her private office, she took a seat behind her desk and tried a tentative smile.

The man smiled slightly in return, but something about his response unnerved her—and it had nothing to do with sexuality, either his or hers. It was more the feeling that he was a cat preparing to spring on a poor, unsuspecting mouse, and *she* was the mouse.

She cleared her throat. "Do you have any questions before I bring in the collection?"

"No."

His nonchalance, both in the gift shop and here, was adding to her unease. She had expected at least some degree of anger. She excused herself to collect the exhibit tray.

Returning she said, "You'll find everything here. I examined them myself. Nothing seems to have been unduly harmed."

"Nothing inanimate, you mean."

Sonya paused. "Ah, yes." She pulled the cloth from the top of the padded tray and held her breath while he looked at the articles. One by one, his long-fingered hand moved over each piece but lingered longest on the bottle. Then, choosing it above the others, he lifted it from the tray and held it to the light.

Sonya glanced at him curiously. Was he, too, searching for a flash of green?

Quickly she called her mind to order. "Is everything satisfactory?" she asked.

"It seems so." He replaced the bottle in the tray.

Sonya resumed her seat, clinging to her mantle of professionalism. He was sitting so still, watching her so calmly. Did the man have no emotions? Didn't he care that the collection had been found? She resumed her part in the minidrama. "The insurance company has been contacted. In case you aren't aware of procedure in a situation such as this, at the moment, the insurance company owns the collection. When they made payment on the claim, technically, they purchased it. That means that when it reappears..."

"It's theirs," Christian Townsend said.

"Yes. But under the circumstances, we have word that they're willing to sell it back to you. My colleagues and I have discussed the matter, and since the collection isn't all that valuable, we feel it might be best—purely from a financial perspective—to let them keep it. Of course, that decision is up to you."

"Thank you." He paused. "Exactly who found the exhibit?"

Trying not to reveal her passionate desire that the next few minutes be over, Sonya folded her hands on top of her desk. "As you may have noticed, the museum is undergoing a rather extensive renovation. One of the projects is to replace all the out-dated plumbing. When one of the workmen opened a wall to get to a section of pipe, he found what turned out to be the collection hidden inside."

"What's the workman's name?"

Sonya was surprised by the unexpected probe. "Why do you want to know?"

"Just answer, please."

"I can't give you his name!"

"Why not?"

"Because... Because it's private museum bus—" Sonya stopped, calming herself. "What possible purpose would it serve? Everything is very straightforward. The collection was found...you were called, or rather your uncle—" She bit her lip. She shouldn't have mentioned his uncle, because when she did, his handsome features hardened. "We've done everything we possibly could to facilitate..."

"I don't believe you."

Sonya's clasped hands convulsed. The initiative was fast slipping away from her.

He completely shed his detached facade as he leaned forward and said sharply, "You've informed me of two things, Ms. Douglas. One, that I should let the insurance company keep my uncle's collection— something I find wholly appalling. And two, that you'd prefer me to slink out of town without asking any hard questions."

"I didn't..." He *was* angry. She *was* the mouse.

"Oh, but you did," he corrected. "The museum's attitude is exactly the same now as it was thirty years ago. You don't care who gets hurt as long as it's not you. Everyone is supposed to bury their heads and accept what they're told. Well, I'm not going to allow that to happen again, Ms. Douglas. Not this time. I do have questions about what happened, both then and now and I intend to get all the answers."

Sonya moved jerkily away from her desk.

He continued, "Why is it so important that this be kept a secret?"

Sonya remained silent.

"There *are* other people I can ask."

She swung around.

He waited for her answer.

She was being pushed into a corner. If she didn't give him an answer, how far was he prepared to go? She cleared her throat. "Recently...we've had some—some rather troubling difficulties. All fabrication, of course. But . . . we've been hurt."

"So the museum is in trouble again and as before, you and your *colleagues* are willing to do anything to protect it."

"Not anything!" she denied. The way he put it sounded dreadful.

"Out of loyalty?" he asked.

"Is that so terrible?"

"I wouldn't be surprised if it was something more basic, like jobs . . . and money."

Sonya wanted to order him from her office. It was one thing to demand the truth and another to be insulting. But remembering what Ted had said and remembering the importance of her role in protecting the museum's reputation, she forced her voice not to quaver with anger as she said, "I'm doing everything in my power to be civil to you, Mr. Townsend. I've explained the situation—much deeper than I had planned. I'm sorry the collection was lost and I'm even sorrier that it was found. But since it *was* found, we'll have to decide what to do about it. Now, you can create a scene and cause trouble for the museum or you can accept our heartfelt apology, take your collection and go. It's as simple as that. There's nothing more I can say."

"There is another alternative," he contradicted softly. "You can help me find out who did it in the first place. That's what *I* want, Ms. Douglas. You're right, the collection in itself isn't valuable. It never was, but it *was* important to my uncle. It broke his heart when the pieces were lost. They held great sentimental value for him.

"All that time ago when we came to your precious museum, no one was interested in discovering the truth. Everyone wanted to sweep the incident under the rug. They even tried to place the blame on an innocent man, but it didn't work. Now today, all I've gotten from you since I came is another sweep job. I want to learn the truth, Ms. Douglas. I *intend* to find the truth—and I can do it with your help or without it. You choose."

His ultimatum held the bitter sting of promise.

After a moment Sonya said, "I'll find the workman's name. Will that do?"

"It's a start." This time when he smiled, it was more fully formed and held both a dashing recklessness and enough sex appeal to penetrate even Sonya's distracted state.

She felt herself responding, then instantly clamped down on her reaction. He was a hateful man, one she could very happily do without. She was only helping him because she was forced to.

She reached for the telephone and began to punch in a number, but her finger slipped and she had to start over again . . . with him watching.

Querulous tears formed in her eyes. She had known this was going to be an absolutely horrible day.

Chapter Four

"He's meeting with him this morning. What do I do?"

"Go with him. If he says he wants your help, give it to him. Be his second skin."

"I can't do that!"

Ted Armstrong smiled. "Can you think of a better way to control the situation?"

"Ted—"

"In particular keep him away from Millicent What's-her-name. She'd have a field day with him."

"But what about my work? I can't do all that and keep..."

"When you're sick, what happens? Someone else takes your place. And when you're on vacation— That assistant of yours, Barbara, she's done very well in the past. Take whatever time you need. Help him in any way that doesn't hurt the museum. Then get rid of him."

"But—"

"Are you trying to tell me you're not capable?" When Sonya didn't answer, he stood up. "Stick to him like glue. That's the only advice I can give you."

With that he pushed her into the hall.

Before the door was shut, she saw that he had started to grin.

CHRISTIAN STARED INTENTLY at the glowing screen. A thirty-year-old headline blared back at him: A Question of Trust—Museum in Hot Water. His gaze scanned the follow-up below, which included an interview with the then museum director, Raymond McArthur, who denied any and all culpability on the part of his institution. Christian made a note of his name. The police commissioner was also quoted: "The perpetrator would be caught!" Christian noted Commissioner Donald Squires's name as well before switching to the microfilmed record of the next day's newspaper. In it there was no further mention of the theft. Then starting two days later, there was a regular series of lurid headlines and stories. Museum Rocked by Scandal—Contributors Grow Uneasy, Another Black Mark on SF History, and Christian's favorite, Corruption in the Crypt!

He read each article, being sure to list each name mentioned and that person's connection with the disappearance. Finally he came upon: Owner Arrives—Blames Museum, Driver Arrested—Claims Innocence, McArthur Agrees—Driver Did It!

Christian remembered those last stories. He had read them as a child and tried to understand. As an adult, he read them again, and was still not enlightened except by the fact that Raymond McArthur seemed very sure that the driver, Tomas Delia, had done it. The man was a temporary employee who had been hired the week before. Uneducated and recently let go from his previous job, he was a perfect scapegoat. No wonder Uncle Dominic had been suspicious.

Christian stretched and glanced at his watch. His interview with the workman was in less than a half hour. Quickly he scanned the following days' articles, which chronicled the flimsy evidence, the harassment of the driver's family and friends and finally, the man's release from jail. Then, after replacing the last square of film in its protective folder, he switched off the machine and was preparing to stand up when the librarian who had assisted him earlier paused at his side.

"Did you find everything you need?" she asked, her voice muted but friendly.

"I believe so."

"Oh, that's good then. I wanted to tell you that if you needed to know more about that time period, I've just remembered that one of our own people might be able to help. Her husband was a reporter for one of the local papers and was deeply involved with the story of the exhibit's disappearance. You probably read some of his articles. He was really quite good."

Christian smiled warmly. "Would you introduce me?"

"Of course."

He was led to a woman sorting returned books onto a cart that was nearly full. She looked up when they approached. An aurora of fine white hair framed a sweetly lined face that mirrored a comfortable resignation to life.

"Flora, if you would please—" The librarian called her away from her work, then handled the introductions and explained Christian's interest in the past. Soon the two were left alone at a nearby study table.

"I never believed the man did it," the woman said softly after a moment of encouragement. "A lot of people did. They thought he'd gotten away with a neat trick when the police didn't find enough evidence. But I didn't. Neither did my Ralph. Not privately."

Christian cocked his head. "Why not?"

"It was all too easy. Also, I knew Mr. Delia's nephew. He was my vegetable boy. He came round every other day and brought me the freshest vegetables. A nice boy. It's really too bad about what happened to the family."

"What happened?"

She shook her head. "They were never the same. Not after a thing like that. Trouble just seemed to follow them."

Christian glanced at his watch again. He had to go. "Would it be all right if I talked to you again, when I have more time?"

"Of course, whenever you like. I'm here most days. I do a lot of volunteer work. It keeps me busy."

Christian voiced his thanks. He knew that not everyone would be as forthcoming. Some, if not most, would much prefer to forget the whole incident, like the people at the museum. Which brought thoughts of Sonya Douglas to mind. Would she be any more willing to cooperate today than she had been yesterday? Somehow he doubted it.

A smile touched his lips at the prospect.

SHE WAS PLANTED FIRMLY at the table when Christian arrived at the museum's garden café.

"Museum policy," she explained.

He didn't believe her, but he didn't challenge the excuse. He settled easily into his chair. "Here to take notes?" he teased.

"No," she answered stiffly.

The workman, wearing stained overalls, squirmed in his seat. He was not at all comfortable in such elegant surroundings. The artistic theme of the museum had been continued outdoors with prints of the masters hung on rock walls and bronze sculptures interspersed throughout a profusion of green plants. A cascading waterfall even took up one corner of the courtyard.

They were not alone in taking advantage of the café's ambience. Several expensively clad patrons were occupying nearby tables.

Christian extended his hand to the man. "My name is Christian Townsend. And you're . . . ?"

The man wiped his palm on his overalls before accepting the greeting. "Smith. Nolan Smith."

Christian's smile was easy. "I'd like to ask you a few questions, if you don't mind, Nolan. Ah—would you like something to eat?"

Nolan shook his head.

Christian turned to Sonya. "Would you?" She, too, declined.

Christian shrugged and ordered coffee and a roll. "I didn't have breakfast this morning, so I'm not going to let the opportunity pass."

Sonya wanted him to get on with the interview. The café was on friendly ground, but it was still a public place. Christian took time to stir sugar into his cup. "Being a plumber must be hard work," he observed.

Nolan nodded.

"Long hours."

Again Nolan nodded.

Finally arriving at his point, Christian said, "You found some objects the other day."

The man hunched forward. "Is something missing? Because if it is, I didn't take it. I saw those things and called my supervisor right away!"

"No, nothing's missing."

"Are you a cop?"

Christian laughed, finding the idea amusing. "Not at all."

"Security, then?" This time when Christian did nothing to disabuse him of the idea, the plumber continued, "I've got a wife...kids. I can't lose this job!"

"No one said anything about you losing your job. I'm just curious. How did the wall look before you opened it?"

Nolan Smith frowned. "Like a wall."

"There was nothing different about it?"

"Not that I remember."

"Are you sure?"

The man scratched his head. "Well, there could have been a patch, I suppose. A spot that was a little different shade...lighter, you know."

"But it didn't stand out?"

"No. If it was a patch, it was a darn good one."

Christian reached into his pocket and withdrew several bills, which he carefully folded and extended across the table to the other man. The action was smooth and carried out so as not to call attention to the participants. "Thank you for your trouble, Mr. Smith. I appreciate it."

Nolan shot Sonya a quick look. Christian saw him and urged, "It's okay, take it." The bills instantly disappeared.

With a widening grin, the plumber stood up. "If you can think of anything else I can help you with, you let me know. You hear?"

"I will," Christian promised.

As the man hurried off, Sonya pushed away from the table. "I don't see what good that did."

Christian leaned back in his chair. "Oh?"

"I certainly didn't hear him say anything important."

"There was a wall patch. He saw it. I've checked . . . that was an original wall, built when the museum first opened. Almost a hundred years ago, correct?"

"Yes."

"So the wall would have to have been patched—"

Sonya interrupted impatiently. "Otherwise the collection couldn't have been put there. Yes. So?"

He smiled. "I'll turn you into my Watson yet."

Sonya counted to five. Why had she opened her mouth to berate Ted? If she had kept quiet, *he* would be the one dealing with this man. Not her.

Christian Townsend's smile grew at her obvious displeasure, and the effect of that smile on Sonya irritated her even more. She was *not* susceptible to this man. Just because he was one of the most handsome men she had ever seen in her life didn't mean a thing. Not a thing. Anyway, how a person looked meant absolutely nothing to her. She was impervious. She diverted her gaze.

"If it was such a perfect patch job," he continued, deciding not to tease her any longer, "then that means that whoever hid the collection had plenty of time to do it. They didn't have to hurry or take the chance of making it visible, which lets off anyone from outside the museum. It was an inside job, as my uncle suspected."

Sonya's gaze jerked back. She hadn't thought of that! Quickly she jumped to the defense. "Oh, surely not. What would be the motive?"

"That's what I plan to find out. Have you decided to help?"

Sonya cursed the entire situation. If only she'd known what she was in for when she came back to the museum the night of the discovery, *she* would have been the one to suggest repatching the hole without saying a word. But as it was, she was the designated keeper of the grail. "What do you need?" she asked with more grit than grace.

"The name of each museum employee at that time, especially those still working here today."

"Surely you don't suspect one of them! No, I don't believe it."

"I suspect everyone."

"Even me?"

"You wouldn't have been in diapers yet. But I'm not so sure that you aren't going to try to stop me from finding the truth."

"Then why ask for my help?"

"Because I don't have anyone else."

"Why is it so important to you? I'm sorry to have to say this...but your uncle is dead. It can't matter to him any longer."

"It matters to me."

"Don't you have a job to get back to or something?" she asked without much hope.

"My job can wait."

"Just like mine. All right, I'll get the list. Is there anything else?"

"Not for the moment. On the other hand, you might sit down and have breakfast with me."

Sonya stared at him, surprised into momentary speechlessness. Finally, words tumbled back into her mind, but the only ones she uttered were a stiff, "No, thank you. I have things to do."

Christian opened the roll that had been delivered moments before. "If you look like that too often, your face will stick. My mother used to tell me that when I was little and I believed her."

"You must have been a very gullible child."

Gullibility was never a description that fit any part of his life. "No, I was always considered quite precocious."

"That explains it then."

"What?"

"Your conceit."

Christian choked on his bite of roll. When he recovered, she was gone, and he had the alarmed attention of everyone at the nearby tables.

SONYA THREW HER PURSE on the couch seconds after arriving home. Her jacket soon followed. If she had to live through very many more days like this one— He had been in her hair the rest of the afternoon, asking question after question. By now he knew as much about the museum's inner workings as she did. She even had given him use of a procedure manual to keep him happy.

The telephone rang. She tried to ignore it. "Hildie?" she called. Her sister was the one who received most of the calls in the household. "Hildie, are you there?" The phone continued to ring. Sonya admitted defeat and hurried to answer it. "Yes? Hello?"

"I can't read the notes on page twenty-nine. They look like Sanskrit."

Sonya immediately recognized the voice. She knew she should have listened to her first instinct when he asked for her home phone number. "I thought you said you were through for the day."

"I'm bored."

"And I'm tired."

"I'm the one who should be tired. I'm still suffering from jet lag."

"So what am I supposed to do? Make chicken soup?"

"That's an idea!"

"No."

He sighed.

When he said nothing more, Sonya snapped, "I really am tired. It's been a long day. A very long day. Now if you don't mind, I'm going to toss myself a nice little salad, put my feet up and rest. And you— You can..."

He interrupted with a laugh. "Don't say it."

"I was going to advise that you do the same."

"Sure you were."

"I'm going to hang up now."

"All right, maybe I'll do what you say. But tomorrow, first thing, I want to talk with you."

"I can't wait."

He laughed again and hung up, leaving Sonya to stare at the receiver.

That was the way Hildie found her when she arrived home a minute later. Her sister frowned. "Sonya? Is something wrong?"

Sonya blinked. She had never been hung up on or done the dirty deed to anyone else. She had been taught better manners! She closed her mouth, which she hadn't known was open, and slammed the receiver back on its cradle. "Of all the nerve!"

"You sound like the heroine of a trash novel," her sister teased, coming farther into the room and adding her jacket and books to the pile on the couch.

"What do you know about it?" Sonya snipped.

"Only what I read. Seriously, what's up?"

Sonya wanted to let her temper steep. She suspected that she was using it as a defense mechanism, so the longer she was able to sustain her aggravation, the better. But none of this was Hildie's fault. She was the only innocent in the entire situation. Sonya crossed the room to put an arm around Hildie's shoulders and gave her a hug. "Nothing really. A hard day at work. That's all."

"Who was that on the phone?"

"A very difficult man."

Hildie was instantly interested. "A new boy-friend?"

God forbid! "No. Just someone from the museum."

"Does he have something to do with your sudden burst of overtime?"

"No. Yes. I don't want to think about it, okay? Not now. It's enough to have to deal with him at work."

"Is he new?"

"You could say that."

Sonya wanted to change the subject. "How did it go at the Institute today?"

Now it was Hildie's turn to evade. She walked to the refrigerator and withdrew a soda. "Okay."

"Just okay?"

Her sister shrugged, her expression indicating she didn't want to discuss it. Sonya knew the feeling. To help them both along that avenue, she suggested, "How about a pizza for dinner tonight?"

Hildie lifted stricken eyes. "I was supposed to make dinner again and forgot!"

Sonya shook her head. "It doesn't matter. I think I'd rather have pizza."

Her sister was relieved. "Me, too."

"With everything on it?"

"Definitely."

"You call. I've had enough of phones today."

"You're on!"

While Hildie placed their order, Sonya retrieved their jackets. But before hanging them up, and when she no longer could be seen, she leaned her forehead against the cool closet door. She was tired. She hadn't been lying. If she could just sleep through the next few days—the next few weeks!—she would be happy. But she didn't think that Christian Townsend would allow it. In fact, she knew he wouldn't.

Chapter Five

The next morning the telephone remained silent, at least as far as the threatened call from Christian Townsend was concerned, and Sonya's nerves began to stretch again. What was the man up to? He had said he wanted to talk with her, and now it was nearly noon and still no call. Was he talking to someone he shouldn't, someone who might make the story public?

She worried a line of freshly mangled paper clips. Should she continue to sit here? She had no way of contacting him, no idea of where he was staying. She had thought to go ask Ted—possibly he knew—but decided against it. He didn't need more ammunition to use against her. And grousing to David was out of the question because he was hosting a special tour for a group of patrons.

Sonya swept the paper clips into her wastebasket. She would wait, concentrate on the work she had to do and put the man from her mind.

But putting him from her mind wasn't so simple. Each time the phone rang she jumped, her heart jerking into double time. Because of the situation, she told herself, not for any other reason.

She had turned to her computer and was concentrating on the amber-tinted entries, when she slowly became aware that someone was standing inside her office.

Expecting it was one of her assistants, Sonya swiveled around, only to see Christian Townsend filling her doorway. She watched with wide, unblinking eyes as he moved to the desk a short space behind her and hitched a casual seat along its edge.

"Good morning," he said, smiling sociably.

Instead of the suit he had worn yesterday, this morning he was dressed in dun-colored slacks, a pristine, white shirt, opened at the neck, and a dark blue lightweight jacket. On anyone else the ensemble might have looked ordinary. On him it emphasized his spectacular good looks and his impeccable grooming.

Sonya returned his greeting with a frown. "How did you get back into this section?"

"I walked."

"You're not supposed to be here without permission. It's controlled."

"Have a bad night, did we?"

Sonya was not in the mood. "What kind of night I had is no business of yours."

"It is when you attack me."

"I didn't attack you."

He examined his hands, front and back. "You could have fooled me."

Sonya swung back to the computer. "If that's all you have to say, say it to someone else. I don't have time."

"Do you have the list?"

"It's been ready since eight o'clock this morning." Her tone was even frostier than before.

He smiled. "And so have you. Is that why you're angry with me?"

"I'm not angry."

"This is your typical morning disposition? How do people stand it?"

Sonya's fingers hovered over the keyboard. Was he *trying* to exasperate her? "Let's not get personal, okay?"

"Anything you say."

Sonya hissed beneath her breath.

The silence between them grew. Finally, unable to stand it any longer, she looked back to see what he was doing. He had moved from his perch on her desk to a nearby padded tray and was examining at arm's length a bronze study of a horse. It, along with a companion piece, was waiting to be exhibited.

"Mr. Townsend—" she interrupted.

"Christian," he supplied. "Beautiful workmanship."

"It's very valuable."

"I'll be careful." He turned it from side to side.

When she remained pointedly watchful, a dark brow arched. "I know what I'm doing. My uncle taught me to handle artifacts when I was a child."

"He was free to do as he wished with his own collection. This is *my* responsibility."

"Which you take very seriously."

"Yes."

"Like you take everything else."

"Is there something wrong with that?"

"No, but there is more to life."

"I'm very satisfied with my life."

"Are you?"

"Stop asking so many questions."

"Does it bother you when I do?"

Sonya took refuge in rolling the tray from her office to her top assistant's. "Take this to Andrew, will you? I'm tired of waiting for him to come get it."

Barbara immediately stepped away from what she was doing. Her dark hair was pulled into a long, thick rope that hung down her back, and her almond-shaped eyes showed both her quick intelligence and her family's Asian heritage. "Sure thing," she said. "Is something wrong?"

Sonya drew an exasperated breath. "Why is every-one always asking me if something is wrong? Nothing is wrong. Everything is fine. Just fine!"

Barbara winced. "Sorry I asked. Is Andrew in his office?"

"I don't know where he is."

"I'll find him, then. Don't get upset."

"I am *not* upset!"

Barbara left her office shaking her head.

Sonya, seeing the situation as it had been played, leaned against a tall metal file cabinet and told herself that she had to regain control. She couldn't let Christian Townsend get to her so easily, not if she was going to attain her needed goal.

After arranging her expression to one of serene ability, she returned to her office. But he was gone, which caused her to move into action, her expression no longer serene. She had to find him! She would not go through the rest of the day as anxiously as she had spent the morning. The man might be difficult to be around, but he was equally difficult when he was not there for her to see what he was doing. And he could be *doing* anything. He didn't seem to think that rules were made for him.

She caught up with him in the museum proper, not far from the doorway that led to her underground lair. His attention had been caught by a collection of objects housed in a tall glass showcase. She forced herself not to rush to his side. Instead, she approached him sedately. He didn't notice. She was at his side for several awkward seconds before he turned. His surprise at her presence was genuine.

"I didn't mean for you to leave," she murmured.

"I know when to make a strategic retreat, unlike those poor devils." He motioned to the pen-and-ink sketches depicting the battle between two Spanish galleons, whose treasures had been discovered off the coast of Florida some years before. Both ships had fought then lay in deadly silence until a consortium of archaeologists and independent investors had brought their story back to life. Several gold coins, a jeweled goblet and a number of religious articles from the ships were displayed in the secured case.

Sonya glanced at the exhibit before returning to the subject she thought more important. "I haven't given you the list."

He shrugged lightly. "Hang on to it. I don't need it yet. I have an appointment."

"You mean, after all the work I did—"

He looked at her. "I made some calls this morning. That's why I was late." At her start, he said, "Don't worry. I haven't said anything incriminating to anyone ... yet."

"Who— Who is your appointment with?"

"You don't trust me an inch, do you? But then I can't say that I blame you. I wouldn't trust me, either."

Sonya said nothing.

He smiled. "I'm meeting with the widow of the man who was accused of stealing my uncle's collection. She's agreed to see me at her house at one." He waited for the impact of his words to register. "I suppose you'd like to come along."

"Yes, please." Sonya cleared her throat. Had her voice squeaked?

"Can you be ready by twelve-thirty?"

Since it was almost that time now, Sonya nodded. She'd skip lunch today. She didn't feel like eating anyway.

"All right. I'll meet you out front in ... about ten minutes?"

Again Sonya nodded.

He took another long view of the galleons' treasure before moving away.

Sonya quickly retraced her steps to the basement. There was something she had to do. Earlier she had found the file on the exhibit's disappearance—the museum's private news clippings and notes—and she wanted to read through it. Especially where it concerned the driver's widow. She wanted to see what she would be up against.

THE WOMAN PULLED ASIDE A CURTAIN, peeked from behind the safety of glass and stout wrought-iron bars, then let the curtain fall back into place. A moment later the front door was pulled partway open.

Faded gray eyes gazed suspiciously from a weathered face that still retained shadows of a strong-featured attractiveness. Her silver hair was platted and lay in two flat rows across the top of her head.

"Mr. Townsend?" she asked, looking to Christian before allowing her attention to move curiously to Sonya.

"Yes, and this is Sonya Douglas, my assistant. Thank you for letting us come, Mrs. Delia."

As the woman backed away from the door, Christian swung the heavy gate outward and motioned for Sonya to precede him.

The house was overly warm and smelled of collected age. An overstuffed couch and chair, several tables filled with knickknacks and remembrances, a small television set, a hutch and a multitude of cats filled the room. Old-fashioned wallpaper, its bright color dulled, brought little comfort or cheer. Several cats moved, disturbed.

Christian bent to pick one up. The animal with long white hair and exotic blue eyes purred as he stroked it.

"Please sit down," the woman said, shooing other cats from the sofa and chair.

Christian didn't hesitate. The white cat stayed in his arms, seeming to like the magic of his touch. Sonya perched on the opposite chair as the woman did likewise on the cushion next to Christian.

"We're sorry to disturb you, Mrs. Delia," he said.

"I remember you as a little boy. So handsome, even then. Your uncle didn't believe the lies told about my Tomas. I have never forgotten that."

There was more than a slight accent to her words, a link to her native country. Sonya saw that the woman had never blended. She might live in this country, but the small world of her house remained in another.

"Neither have I."

The woman sighed. A yellow cat climbed into her lap and she began to stroke it unconsciously. "So much trouble. Why do you wish to speak of it again? My Tomas is long dead."

"My uncle was an honorable man, Mrs. Delia. All his life he tried to live to the highest ideals. He never cheated, never falsely charged, never lied, and he felt that each of these things was done to your husband. I know for a fact that he was as sorry for what happened to your husband as he was about his collection's disappearance. For the rest of his life it was there in his mind."

"You speak of him as in the past."

"He died three weeks ago." Christian glanced at Sonya, whose eyes had widened with surprise. "He lived a full life."

"Death waits for us all," the woman said, crossing herself and murmuring a silent prayer. When she was through, her faded gaze fixed steadily on Christian. "There still is no answer to my question."

The white cat jumped from Christian's lap and began a light grooming a short distance from his leg.

"I've come to right the wrong," he said simply.

The woman was quiet, then said, "You are a young man. Surely there are other things you wish to do. Let the past lie in the past. Bones that are bleached white are clean."

"I don't agree with that."

The woman looked at Sonya. Sonya felt her eyes move over her. She sat very still under the perusal, her heart thumping quickly because of the intensity of the woman's gaze and because of the information Christian had just imparted. She hadn't known his uncle had died so recently. Somehow—she wasn't sure exactly why—that put a different complexion on the situation.

"Young woman, can you not make him see?"

Sonya's smile was tentative. She was awed by the great strength of will she sensed behind the woman's reserve. It was hard to believe that this was the same person she had read about in the news clippings. Thirty years before, when her husband was taken to jail, the woman had cowered from the police. Sonya remembered the one picture of her that had been printed. Fear had been naked in every line of her face. Time and adversity must have honed something inside her. "He does as he wishes, Mrs. Delia. I have no power over him."

"You could, if you wished to use it."

At her words, Sonya experienced the same sense of eeriness as she had when the tiny glass bottle flashed with green life—as if she were slightly removed from the moment, as if time had somehow shifted.

Christian intervened. "I make my own decisions, Mrs. Delia. I want to bring back the past, to look at it again, to see where the truth lies."

"The secret to a peaceful life is to accept what has happened."

Christian smiled. "I don't search for a peaceful life."

The woman nodded. "No, men of your sort never do." She stood up. "I must rest now."

Christian took the hint and he stood up as well, assisting Sonya from her chair. "May we visit again?" he asked.

"My house is always open to my friends."

THE SLEEK BLACK SPORTS CAR Christian claimed to have rented sat at the curb. A small crowd had collected around it but parted when Christian and Sonya came away from the only neatly kept house in the area. All the others had deteriorated, their paint peeling and much-needed repairs having been either postponed or forgotten.

"Nice car, man," came a smooth compliment.

Sonya's nerves tightened with apprehension. This was not one of the better neighborhoods in the city. Always a working-class area, it now housed more hard-core unemployed and had a reputation for being dangerous. When Christian's hand came out to encircle her arm, she didn't try to pull away.

"Thanks," he replied, and reached for the handle of the passenger door. He was stopped by the long, thin body that refused to get out of the way. The crowd was now watching to see what would happen next.

"Is it yours?" the man blocking the door asked.

"No."

"You steal it?"

Christian grinned. "I'm tempted."

The recklessness of Christian's smile drew an answering smile from their provocateur. One brigand recognizing another? Sonya wondered.

"Let me know if it gets too hot," the man said. "I know a man who can make it worth your while."

"I'll remember that."

The long body shifted. "Nice taste in ladies, too."

Sonya stiffened. Christian's hand tightened in warning on her arm. As the door cleared, he saw her inside. When she could no longer hear what was being said, he murmured something that made the other man laugh.

The crowd stepped away as Christian got into the car and started the engine. In the exact opposite of what the situation could have become, the tall thin man waved them away, a wide grin making his face look far less threatening.

Sonya shifted her wide-eyed gaze to Christian. "What did you *say* to him?"

Christian didn't look away from the street ahead. "I told him you weren't a lady."

Sonya blinked. Having lived in San Francisco for a few years, she wasn't sure exactly how to take that explanation. "You mean . . . as in I'm not female?"

Christian laughed. "I hadn't thought of it that way! No, I didn't mean that."

Sonya's eyes widened even more. "Then you meant . . ."

"I said what I had to say to get us out of there. Would you rather still be standing there?"

"No."

"Then?"

"I still don't like it."

"I can circle around and drop you off."

She adjusted her skirt over her knees and didn't answer.

Christian shot her an amused glance and kept the engine purring steadily forward.

Sonya fumed to herself. This was above and beyond the call of duty. She wasn't *paid* to put up with the likes of him.

A few minutes later his voice broke into her thoughts. "When you're through sulking, how about something to eat?"

"I'm not sulking."

"Thinking, then."

"I'm not hungry."

"I am."

"Is food such an important part of your life?"

"Among other things."

Sonya would not be drawn to ask what the "other things" were because he might tell her! "I really should get back to the museum."

"I have another appointment."

Sonya groaned inwardly. "Who with this time?"

"A librarian..."

"How interesting."

"...whose husband was a reporter on one of the local papers thirty years ago. He wrote most of the articles concerning the theft."

"How interesting!"

"I thought you'd change your tune."

"You don't mind if I tag along?"

"Could I get rid of you if I tried?"

Now it was Sonya's turn to smile sweetly.

THE SPECIALTY OF THE RESTAURANT Christian took her to was crab, and since it was in season, the place was packed.

Their table was barely large enough for one, much less two, and their elbows were on friendly terms with other diners' elbows. But everyone was happy and conversation flowed around them.

In the general din, Sonya thought it safe to probe. "Why didn't you tell me your uncle had died recently?"

"Would it have made a difference?"

"I would have understood the situation better."

"Why's that?"

"Do you have to ask?"

"I think so."

She shrugged. "Because... Well, different people have different ways of mourning."

"You think I'm only doing this because of my uncle's death?"

"Aren't you?"

He sat back in his chair, ducking when a waiter pivoted and swung a loaded tray over his head. "I'm doing it because I believe it's the right thing to do."

"How old was your uncle?"

"He would have been ninety-seven on his next birthday."

"Wow."

"He was my paternal grandfather's oldest brother."

"It gets complicated."

"My entire family is complicated."

Sonya stirred sugar into her coffee. "In what way?"

It was odd, but in these surroundings, with this swell of humanity around them, she felt less intimidated by him. He didn't seem quite so overwhelming, so overpowering. Still, she wasn't unaware of the looks a number of women at other tables were giving them...at Christian because of the way he looked and at her because she was with him. It was her own private little joke that they were probably wondering what in the world she was doing with him. Under other circumstances, the two of them would never have been together.

"I have three older sisters and my parents, each considered crazy in their own way."

"Who considers them crazy?"

"The rest of the world."

"Did you drive them over the edge?"

He smiled. "You think I could?"

"I think you're capable of it, yes."

"It's a miracle they haven't done the same to me."

"Don't be so sure they haven't."

His smile broadened, and Sonya's breath fairly stopped in her throat. When he looked at her like that, she felt it all the way to her toes.

"One of my sisters is off in the Sahara, doctoring camels this time, I believe. Another is in Borneo, researching a documentary. The third I just left in London, possibly ending a long-term affair with a Russian émigré. And my parents...my parents are somewhere in Australia. God knows where exactly. Just your ordinary, everyday family."

"What about you? When you're not here shaking up the past, what do you do?"

"This and that."

"What exactly?"

"I harass beautiful women."

"Besides that."

"Isn't that good enough?"

"Not to make a living."

"I don't need to make a living."

"Next you're going to tell me you're filthy rich."

"Would that disappoint you?"

Sonya had been teasing, but suddenly she saw that he wasn't. She quickly straightened, glancing at her watch. "What time is the appointment?"

"You didn't answer my question."

She stood up.

His chair's legs scraped against the floor. "I told her about three."

It was a little after two. "Which library?"

"The main one, near city hall."

"What are we going to do in the meantime? That will take all of ten minutes to get to."

"I thought we'd take a walk along the Embarcadero."

"How do you know San Francisco so well?"

"I've lived here from time to time. My family has a home."

"One of several, I suppose."

Christian didn't reply.

As Sonya made her way out of the restaurant, she didn't understand why his family's wealth irritated her. Maybe it was because she and Hildie always seemed to have such a hard time making ends meet. Maybe it was because the glitterari of San Francisco had always repulsed her with their callousness to the needs of the many around them: See a beggar, turn your head. Conspicuous consumption was not an attribute in her eyes.

Christian caught up with her as she walked along the street. Without conscious thought, she was heading toward the Bay several streets over, toward the area he had mentioned.

His fingers snaked round her arm as he matched her steps to his. Neither spoke.

A fish smell wafted through the air. Tourists, what there were of them in February, huddled against the cold. For some reason, even in winter, people thought that San Francisco was warm. They didn't realize it was the rainy season and that the cold could be bitter. They also didn't realize that summer was little better, except that there was no rain.

When the light mist turned into a steady rain, Christian pulled her into the doorway of a souvenir shop. On the counter by the door was a grouping of key chains like those sold in the museum. Catching her eye, he set the chains clinking.

Averting her gaze, she was shocked when a finger touched her chin and brought her head back around. It was warm and strong and very determined.

Of necessity, they were standing close together. Others, too, had taken refuge in the shop. His midnight-blue eyes, guarded by long black lashes, were looking down at her. For a long moment, he said nothing.

Sonya wanted to look away but found that she couldn't.

When he spoke, his voice played almost directly into her ear, swirling along the nerve endings, making her body tingle. "Don't be angry," he murmured.

She swallowed, trying to fight the feeling that was enveloping her. "Why not?" she whispered.

"I'm not sure."

Sonya wanted him to kiss her, right there in the shop, in front of everyone. She wanted it with a sudden passion that she hadn't known she possessed. As his head began to lower, hers tilted in accommodation. Then she remembered who she was and who he was and the spell was shattered into a thousand tiny unmatched pieces. She looked quickly away, battling down the urge to escape. Only the rain gave her a second thought, holding her in place, which let him regain the upper hand.

"Why did you do that?" he questioned softly.

She refused to look at him. "I didn't do anything."

"I know."

A child jostled her as he played, bored with his confinement. Sonya glanced at his mother, who had been staring at Christian. Embarrassment colored the woman's cheeks when she realized that she had been caught.

Sonya wanted to tell her that she was free to look . . . that she didn't have any hold on the man she was with. But the words wouldn't leave her lips. There was no use making an already bad situation even worse.

Christian stepped over to another counter, slipped money to the attendant for the umbrella he had chosen, then made his way back to Sonya. "Come on. Let's go."

One umbrella meant they had to walk side by side, but before long the rain stopped and the umbrella was put away.

Sonya was careful not to get too near to him again. She was already going to have a hard time explaining the afternoon to herself. She didn't want to have to try to explain any more.

Chapter Six

In her quiet way, the volunteer at the public library loved to talk. She started off on the subject of the theft, but soon got sidetracked to her grandchildren and the exorbitant cost of real estate in the city.

Christian let the woman rattle on, while periodically glancing at Sonya, who didn't seem to be hearing any of it. Her features were expressionless, her eyes slightly glassy.

When the librarian paused before launching into another topic, Christian nodded, and soon her words were flowing around him again, though almost immediately they began to lose purchase. Without conscious will, his thoughts returned to the souvenir shop and the moment when the earth seemed to take a halting breath.

Silence snapped his attention back to the small room and the woman sitting across from him at the narrow table.

Flora Richards was embarrassed but bravely trying to smile past it. "I'm so sorry," she said. "My Ralph used to tell me I'd talk Saint Peter to death at the Pearly Gates, if given half a chance!"

Christian murmured, "Saint Peter would be charmed."

"That's not what Ralph—" The woman hushed, pleased at the idea of the handsome young man thinking that she was in any way charming. Her smile grew in warmth. "Now, where was I before I got distracted?"

"You were telling us about Tomas Delia."

"Oh, yes!" She glanced at Sonya, who still was deep in reverie, and a tiny frown creased her brow.

Christian, seeing the woman's concern, gave Sonya's ankle a light tap beneath the table. She jumped as if she had been shot, and when she realized that both of her companions were looking at her, a light blush stole up her cheeks.

"Tomas Delia?" Christian reminded Flora, directing the librarian's attention back to the proper subject.

Sonya moved uncomfortably in her chair. She hadn't realized her attention had slipped away. One moment she had been listening to the woman's voice droning on about her grandchildren's favorite television show, then somehow she was reliving the moment when she would have given anything in the world to be swept into Christian Townsend's arms.

She wiggled in her chair again, becoming even more uncomfortable. Christian glanced at her and winked before returning his attention to the librarian. Did he know? Did he have any idea?

Sonya forced herself to concentrate on what the woman was revealing.

"...so, as I said, my Ralph was suspicious. He never liked pat answers. After Mr. Delia was released and things began to settle down, he was planning to do another story. He had some kind of lead, but he was pushed on to another assignment. Then he got sick, and everything sort of got lost from that point on. No one wanted to hear about the story when he asked to do it again some years later. He was told to 'let sleeping dogs lie.' His editor's exact words."

Christian had straightened. "What kind of lead? Do you know?"

The woman shrugged. "I have no idea. Ralph didn't like to talk about the details of any article he was developing. He thought it was bad luck."

"Did he keep notes?"

The librarian laughed. "I have a whole garage full of his notes! He didn't like to throw things like that away. But if I wanted to keep an empty can or bottle, I never heard the end of it, God rest his soul."

"Would it be possible for us to look through those notes?"

The woman suddenly became more guarded. "Why?"

Sonya tapped Christian on the ankle, reminding him to be careful. He looked almost as startled by the act as she had, but he covered his surprise better. There was no embarrassment. *He* hadn't been caught thinking what she had.

"I'm interested in the case, Mrs. Richards, you know that. Any information you could provide would be appreciated."

"Are you writing a story of your own?"

"No, but I want the truth found."

The woman gazed at him steadily. "I'll have to check with my son. Technically, my husband left his papers to him. I'll have to see what he says before I can—"

"I understand."

"I'm not trying to be difficult. You seem like a very nice young man, and you too, miss. It's just—"

"We're not the least offended, Mrs. Richards. Check with your son and then give me a call at this number." Christian jotted a number down on a pad that was sitting on the table. He tore off the top sheet and handed it to the woman. The smile he bestowed on her wiped away any remaining awkwardness from the moment. Sonya saw the woman melt.

"I'm sure Donald will agree," she said.

"I'll be waiting for your call."

HE INSISTED UPON taking her home once he discovered that she didn't have to go back to the museum. Why she hadn't thought of a reason to return to the museum's safety, Sonya didn't know. The truth had just slipped out.

The black sports car purred to a stop in front of her house. And wouldn't you know? In a city where it was practically unheard of to find a parking place anywhere within the first half hour of searching for one, a spot was vacated and he was first in line to take it.

"You don't need to get out," she said, already pushing herself free.

The engine was cut and he stepped out. "Nonsense. I'll see you to your door."

"We're not getting back from a date. There's no need."

He cocked his head, his black hair being blown slightly out of place by the breezes from the Pacific. "Are you trying to hide a husband or something?"

"A husband! I'm not married."

"Glad to hear it. So why won't you let me see where you live?"

"Because I don't see any reason to."

"You're not being very friendly."

"I'm not *paid* to be friendly."

"Ever the loyal museum employee."

"I don't see why you have to be so nasty about that."

"I'm a natural skeptic."

"About everything and everyone?"

"I've found it's usually very healthy to remain a little skeptical."

"Like not making a practice of dancing on the sharp edge of a sword."

Christian narrowed his eyes. He stopped her progress up the stairs. "Why did you say that?"

"I don't know. It seemed to fit."

As he continued to study her, blood began to race through Sonya's veins. His mouth was so beautifully formed, so virile and warm looking.

She jerked her arm away and climbed the remaining stairs to the landing. He came right behind her.

"You're a strange woman, Sonya Douglas."

"Thank you," she snapped.

His laughter caused tingly goose bumps to break out over her skin. She determined it was due to the dampness in the air.

"I meant that as a compliment," he said.

"I'll try to remember."

He caught her arm again. Once again she jerked it away. "Don't *do* that!"

Her eyes were alive with indignation. His were bright with amusement. Then something passed between them, like a swiftly moving shadow across a harvest moon. And his head bent... until their lips met, moved away, then met again in the kiss that once had been promised but denied.

Sonya's knees went suddenly weak as a sensuality unlike any she had ever known brought her to a vivid awareness of life. She experienced his touch, the taste of his breath, the scent of his cologne. The sky, even though she couldn't see it, had to be bluer, the air, much, much sweeter. Then he was pulling away and a warm bemusement was coloring his expression.

"I'm glad you're not married," he murmured.

Sonya did everything in her power to collect her scattered wits. She couldn't believe this was happening! She withdrew her hands from his shoulders—heaven only knew when she had put them there!—and stammered, "I—I have to go." She berated herself for her show of weakness, but she couldn't help it; she was totally unnerved.

Without warning, the door behind them swept open, revealing Hildie, who was dragging on her jacket. When her sister saw them, she stopped, her startled gaze going from Sonya to Christian, then back to Sonya again.

Sonya's cheeks were ablaze with embarrassment.

Aware that she had happened upon something sensitive, a slow, elfin grin spread over Hildie's pretty face. "Maybe I should go back in and come out again. I didn't mean to interrupt."

"You didn't interrupt!" Sonya denied quickly.

"That might be a good idea," Christian agreed, ignoring Sonya's words.

Hildie's grin widened as she started to shut the door, but Sonya prevented her by stalking over the threshold. "I'm coming inside!"

Christian slipped through the doorway immediately after her. "And who might you be?"

"Hildie Douglas, Sonya's sister. And you?"

"Christian Townsend."

"Nice name."

"Thanks." He smiled.

"Nice rest of you, too."

"Hildie!"

"I'm only saying what I think! There's no law against that."

Sonya dragged a hand through her hair then turned to her unwelcome guest. "You've seen me inside. Now go. Please."

"Sonya!" Hildie cried in mock imitation of her earlier dismay.

"Hildie, be quiet."

"Would you like a ride to the museum in the morning?" he asked, staying very firmly in place.

"No, I would not."

"You don't live that far out of the way."

"Where would you be driving from?"

"Pacific Heights."

"That fits." He had named one of the most exclusive residential areas in the city. "No, you're totally across town. Don't be ridiculous."

"I like to drive in the city."

"A man after my own heart!" Hildie approved.

Sonya hissed. "Weren't you on your way somewhere?"

"Just over to Patricia's."

"Then why don't you go?"

"It's more fun here at the moment."

"Hildie!"

The tone was one of Sonya's best mother imitations, putting a wealth of warning into one word.

Hildie immediately knew that she had pushed the situation far enough. "I'll be back by six."

When Sonya made no reply, Hildie escaped, calling, "Bye!" over her shoulder.

Christian followed her retreat with laughing eyes. Then, turning, he examined the neatly kept room. It was bright and cheerful, with pale blues, greens and yellows accenting the predominant white. "Nice."

"We try," Sonya muttered, displeased that he was still there. She had a lot to think about and she couldn't begin the process while he was present.

"How old is your sister?"

"Much too young for you."

He glanced at her dryly. "I wasn't thinking that."

Sonya wished she hadn't made the remark. To compensate, she answered, "Almost nineteen."

"She's a cute kid."

"Why don't you tell her that sometime?"

A dark eyebrow arched in inquiry. "She'd hit me?"

"She might."

"Then she's a lot like you."

"I've never hit you."

"You've wanted to. Just like you do right now."

"Well, if you weren't so..."

"Charming?"

"That wasn't the word I was looking for."

His smile grew easier. "What if I told you you're an 'interesting' lady? Would you like that better than 'strange'?"

Sonya shed her jacket, laying it over the back of the couch. It gave her something to do. She'd like to order him from the house, but if he wouldn't go, she didn't know what she could do to make him. "I don't know why you have such a fixation on me."

"I'm wondering about that myself."

"Well, stop!"

He moved casually about the room, examining some of the decorative touches she and Hildie had collected over the years: a colorful egg from the Murano glassworks near Venice, a brass dragon with a clawed foot raised challengingly in the air. "I'm not so sure I can," he mused.

She yanked her jacket off the couch and marched to the closet. "You're here to find the truth about what happened to your uncle's collection, remember? Once you discover that, you're going to leave...to do whatever it is that you do." The hanger scraped against the rod as she replaced it.

When she turned, she was startled to find that he had come up close behind her.

"Why do I frighten you?" he asked quietly.

"You don't."

"Oh, but I do."

"It's only your imagination."

His hand came out to touch her cheek. She trembled. "See?" he said.

"I got a chill outside." Sonya clung desperately to any reason other than the obvious one. The room felt so alive with him in it, almost as if it were vibrating.

"Then maybe we should do something to get you warm," he suggested.

"No!"

Christian didn't move. "Why do I frighten you?" he repeated.

Sonya twisted her hands. "You don't—"

He leaned forward to kiss the tip of her nose teasingly, forcing a change in atmosphere, making it lighter. "I'll see you tomorrow morning. Don't let the bed bugs bite."

He didn't wait for a reply.

When she was alone, Sonya dropped weakly onto the couch. The house was positioned close to a fault line. That had to be why she had felt the earth shake so violently... why it was still shaking.

HILDIE PEERED AT HER from behind the glossy pages of a fashion magazine as Sonya pretended to concentrate on the carrots she was slicing for a salad. "You're sure I can't help?"

"I'm doing fine," Sonya returned. Several more cuts, then she felt Hildie's gaze return. She knew that eventually she was going to have to face her sister's questions, but she wasn't prepared to at the moment. She started to hum, pretending a false state of normalcy.

Hildie put the magazine aside and came to lean her elbows against the opposite side of the counter on which Sonya was working. Reaching out, she popped a carrot piece into her mouth.

Sonya gave her a quick smile and continued humming.

Finally, Hildie could stand it no longer. "Okay," she said, "who's the hunk? Is he that new guy you were talking about the other day, the one you acted like was such a royal pain?"

Sonya's interlude of music stopped; so did the knife. She didn't want to lose a finger. "I said something about a man?"

Hildie smiled. "You certainly did."

Sonya took a breath. "It's not what you think."

"The two of you looked pretty friendly when I opened the door."

"It *wasn't* what you think!"

"What was it then?"

Sonya moved to the refrigerator and extracted the lettuce she had already washed. "He— I—"

"Yes?"

"It was just a silly mistake!"

"Kissing a good-looking man is a mistake? I'll try to remember that the next time I have the opportunity."

"It didn't *mean* anything."

"This gets better and better."

"Hildie, please!"

Her sister's teasing stopped, to be replaced by affronted sensibility. "I don't know what you're so upset about. I've known about the birds and the bees for years now. You told me, remember? Do you think that *I* think you're going to take care of me forever? I'm nearly nineteen, Sonya. Old enough to start taking care of myself. And you're twenty-nine...you should have a life of your own."

"You don't think I have a life of my own?"

"Not really."

The salad was forgotten. "You think I'm not happy?"

"I didn't say that."

"Then?"

"I just think that you should be thinking of getting married...stuff like that. Having kids, you know."

"I'm not interested in that right now."

"Will you ever be? Or have I ruined it for you?"

The edge to her sister's words pulled at Sonya's heartstrings. "You've never ruined anything for me in your life," she assured her, coming around the counter to take hold of her sister's shoulders. "Quite the opposite."

"It couldn't have been any fun doing what you did. You were my age when Mom and Dad got divorced—when you got saddled with me. And it *was* you. Dad tried, but he wasn't very good at being a father. How did you do it?'' Hildie asked.

Sonya thought of the ten long years, when so many times she wasn't sure if she was doing the right thing, especially after their father died. As Hildie said, he wasn't good at being a parent, but at least he had been there to talk to and his advice was often right on the mark. "Dad did more than you think,'' she answered.

"Didn't you ever resent us? I mean, you were young. You must have wanted to go out more often with your friends . . . go to parties and all.''

"I went to some.''

"Not as many as I do.''

Sonya gave Hildie's shoulders a soft shake before releasing her. "I wasn't as much a social butterfly as you, that's true. But we're different people, Hildie. To you it's important to be on the go all the time. I like to kick back and have a quiet evening at home.''

"You have too many quiet evenings at home!''

"Are you telling me I'm a bore?''

Hildie hurried to correct the impression. "Not at all! You're— You've got something, Sonya, but you don't use it enough, that's all. If this man, this Christian guy, thinks you're special, let him. Go out with him. Have a good time and don't be afraid to have him stay overnight, if you want. I'm an adult now, not an impressionable baby. Just remember to use precautions.''

Sonya didn't know whether to laugh or to cry. Her little sister was taking care of *her* now! Is this what it felt like to grow old? And the thought of having to use 'precautions' with Christian Townsend sent her mind reeling.

"I think you're mistaking our relationship. I don't *like* the man, Hildie. Not one little bit."

"He likes you."

Sonya shook her head. "No. Nope. No way."

"He does."

"I only met him two days ago!"

"Sometimes things like that happen fast."

"How do you know so much? Experience?"

"I read," Hildie said in her defence. "And as I've been telling you, I'm not a child any longer."

A teary laugh rose in Sonya's throat which she did nothing to prevent. "I've known that for some time. I'm not trying to keep you little, honey. Really, I'm not."

"I know that."

"But I don't want you to grow up too quickly, either. Enjoy being your age." Now that *did* make her feel old.

Hildie must have thought so, too, because she grinned. "Yes, Grandma."

"And don't sell yourself short."

"Yes, *Great*-grandma."

Watching her sister go contentedly back to her magazine made Sonya shake her head. If only she could resolve her other problems half as easily.

Chapter Seven

David tapped on her office door before entering. "I wasn't sure I'd find you here."

Sonya looked up from the stack of material she was separating into proper filing order. Since Barbara had competently taken over her day-to-day duties, which didn't exactly sit well with Sonya, she was putting her lag time to good use by trying to reduce the backlog of paperwork.

Also, if she was busy, she didn't think, and thinking was definitely not a state in which she wanted to indulge. She had spent most of last night thinking and it had produced nothing but a dull headache and red-rimmed eyes. "I haven't started playing follow the leader yet this morning."

"You look tired," David said, sliding into a spare chair.

"You're just loaded with cheery news, aren't you?"

"In a way. I've just heard that that Townsend fellow is going to buy back the collection. He's already arranged it with the insurance company. So at least that's one problem solved."

"In what way?"

"It won't be our responsibility any longer."

"You think that's going to solve our problem?"

"Why is he so insistent?"

Sonya straightened several loose sheets. "It's a matter of principle to him."

"But it's been thirty years."

"That doesn't seem to matter. He wants to talk to everyone who was in any way involved."

"What's he going to do with the information once he gets it?"

"I have no idea."

"Has he agreed to protect the museum?"

"He hasn't agreed to anything."

"I think you should refuse to help him."

"Would you like to tell that to Ted?"

"Ted has something else to think about at the moment, or so I've heard."

"Oh?"

David leaned closer and motioned for her to follow suit. His voice became hushed. "There's a rumor floating around about a kickback from the D'Arcy Gallery on the Ketchum paintings we exhibited last fall. They sold for a pretty penny at auction, remember?"

"How far has it spread?"

"I heard it from one of the volunteers. The board of trustees will have simultaneous heart attacks when they hear, if they haven't already."

"Has Millicent Walker staked out a spot yet?"

"I haven't seen her."

"Then maybe it's just going around the museum."

"I wouldn't count on it staying private for long."

Sonya grimaced. "No...."

CHRISTIAN PULLED UP SHORT in the doorway, the sight of two blond heads huddled close together greeting him. One belonged to Sonya, the other to a man with a youthful face belied by the spray of silver frost nipping the hair at his temples.

From nowhere, a jolt of jealous anger barreled through him and his first instinct was to swoop across the room, pull the two of them apart and bury his fist in the man's face. As if he were a primal man, ready to fight for his intended mate. That thought shocked him. There was something very different about Sonya Douglas, a difference he couldn't begin to understand yet ... but was she that different?

As he fought to hold himself aloof, neither occupant was aware of his presence. Sonya's face was intent, concerned; the man's showed enjoyment at some revelation.

Regaining his self-control, Christian stepped into the room quoting, "'Gossip is an evil thing by nature...' An ancient Greek poet said that, I believe."

David stiffened at the interruption, his head snapping up.

Sonya recognized the voice and momentarily closed her eyes. Christian's arrival heralded the end of what calm she would find today. She stood up, sensing that she could better protect herself on her feet.

David got to his feet, as well. "I don't know who you think you are..." he began with affronted dignity.

"David," Sonya interrupted, "this is Christian Townsend. Christian, David Pewter, our curator of European art. He—he was the first person on the scene when the collection was found."

Christian's eyes narrowed over the man, looking him up and down. "I'd like to talk to you when you have time."

"My time is limited, especially for frivolities." David was unwilling to back down.

"You don't approve of what I'm doing?"

"It's not my place to approve or disapprove, but you're taking Sonya away from her work."

"She's free to do as she chooses."

"Which is a waste of her training."

"Is it her 'training' you're worried about?"

Sonya thrust herself into the scuffle. The two men had taken an instant dislike to each other and she didn't appreciate having become some kind of verbal football. "I can speak for myself, thank you!"

David's face still held a stubborn edge as he turned to look at her. "If you're not careful, Ted's going to ease Barbara into your position. He's already praising her to high heaven. He says everything is so much more efficient now."

"If the rumor you've heard gets out, it's possible all our jobs will be in jeopardy, so I really can't worry about it." She softened her tone. "Really, David, I can watch out for myself."

His features slowly relaxed until there was a return to his more mild-mannered self. "Your power is deceptive," he murmured.

Sonya had no idea what he meant, but if accepting it without question would settle things down in her office, she would.

"If you need me, you know where I am," David said as he left the room.

Christian's dark blue eyes were alight with amusement. "One of your conquests?"

Sonya scowled. "Leave it alone, okay?"

"I was just wondering."

"You both were obnoxious."

"I notice you didn't award your colors."

"I don't have colors."

"All fair damsels have a scarf, a trinket—"

"Not this one and I'm not particularly fair."

"You have blond hair."

Sonya stacked the papers she had been working on back in the bottom drawer of her file cabinet and asked, "What's on the docket for today?"

He knew exactly what she was doing but allowed himself to be diverted. The line of thought had been played out. There was no gain in pursuing it, especially when he was unsure of his reasons for wanting to play in the first place. And not when he was still trying to figure out his earlier instinctive urge. He had escorted many prettier women than Sonya Douglas in his life, many much more vibrant, more exotic. "Why don't we start by going down the list of people still working here?" he suggested.

Sonya retrieved the needed list from her top desk drawer and as she did, she felt his gaze slide over her. She tried to steel herself for what the day might bring.

CHRISTIAN LIGHTLY SMOOTHED the tip of his shoe into the close-cropped carpeting lining Sonya's office floor. His perch was once again the desk. "That certainly got us nowhere fast."

"I thought we were lucky to find four of them still here."

"All with matching cases of amnesia."

"I sometimes have a hard time remembering what happened yesterday, much less years ago."

"I was watching their eyes. A couple of them knew more than they said."

"Too bad we don't have a rack."

Christian gave a slow smile. "I understand one of my ancestors had more than a passing acquaintance with one of those."

"Somehow that doesn't surprise me."

"He was a pirate. Someone took exception to his methods."

"I wonder if I could rent one for an hour?"

His smile grew. She truly wasn't a beautiful woman. At times she looked almost plain. But at other times, like now, she had a quality that made other women who possessed only beauty seem boringly inane. Her mercurial expression blended laughter with sadness, intelligence with vulnerability, tenderness with a fierce pride. It really was no wonder that he was strongly drawn to her.

Sonya quickly put the distance of the office between them. She had caught his look and felt herself instantly respond. But after last night, she wasn't about to allow any excuse for a repeat performance.

"I could have told you that," she said, referring to his earlier statement. "The people who work for the museum are loyal, especially these people. They have too many years invested here not to be."

"I wasn't asking them if they stole it," he protested. "Just what they remembered. What harm could that do?"

Sonya sighed. "You have to understand. The museum has been going through hard times recently, and now there's probably going to be even more trouble. They're hypersensitive."

"Like you."

She inclined her head.

"Is that what you and Boy Wonder were talking about when I came in?"

"His name is David Pewter. And yes, it was."

"What kind of trouble?"

Sonya wondered if sharing more details of what the museum was experiencing would help. It might, she decided. "Last fall the museum exhibited a grouping of paintings by a fairly unknown artist. Later, when they came up for auction, the price they collected was unusually high. *I* think it's because the artist is talented. Other people might think it's due to something else."

"Like money changing hands."

"Exactly."

"Why doesn't the museum sue if the allegations are false?"

"It's hard to sue the person who starts a rumor. First you have to find him, which isn't easy. Next, the media wiggles loose because they say that they're not doing anything wrong, all they're doing is reporting what's being said. They claim they're not responsible for who's saying it or that source's accuracy. But as any lawyer can tell you, innuendo is his best tool. If doubt can be cast, the jury can't erase it from their mind. It's the same with the public. If enough trust is lost, the donors will hold back on pieces to exhibit—possibly even withdraw exhibits—and patrons will be spooked. Then heads will start to roll, even if no one is at fault." She paused. "At present we're skating on thin ice. If it gets any thinner—"

"There's nothing the museum can do to defend itself?" Christian asked curiously.

"Deny it, that's all."

"You said heads would roll. Yours?"

Sonya shrugged. "Not likely. But some members of the board of trustees are getting impatient. Any more disruptions and Dr. Hockly, our director, will go for sure. Possibly the assistant director, too. You've met him, I believe?" Christian nodded. "And I don't know who else. They could wipe the slate clean, if they wanted."

"That would be a stupid thing to do."

"Yes, but it could happen."

"Don't you have the backing of your patrons?"

"Some of them, yes, but I don't know how long we'll be able to keep it."

Christian lapsed into thought, and Sonya grew uneasy. Possibly she shouldn't have confided in him. What if he decided to use that knowledge as a weapon against them?

His voice was level as he asked, "Are you sure there's not some fire beneath all that smoke?"

Sonya looked at him. "You mean...? No, Dr. Hockly wouldn't do such a thing!"

"What about someone else?"

"I'm telling you, no! Not one thing that's been said is true. I'm sure of it."

"Then someone is purposely trying to destroy the museum...or someone in it. Have you thought of that?"

"It doesn't take a genius. Yes, I've thought of it. But who? And why?"

Christian shrugged and pushed away from the desk, his interest seeming suddenly to change. "I have my own set of problems. I can't get involved in anyone else's. I'd like to see the collection again, please. I've made all the arrangements to buy it back."

Ice tinged Sonya's words at his withdrawal. "Of course." For a moment he had seemed almost sympathetic.

Christian welcomed the distance she was constructing between them. For one crazy second he had wanted to help them, to help the museum that had hurt his uncle so badly and caused him so much grief, and all because of his attraction to a woman.

Sonya walked from the office, her back stiffly erect. She led him past the large work area, the card catalogue and numerous partially filled rows of open shelving. Only when she arrived at a series of flat file cabinets at the back did she stop.

Inside a middle drawer was the collection. Intrigued as he always was since childhood, Christian reached out to touch each piece, his fingers moving lightly over the comb, the cup, the fan...the tiny green bottle.

Sonya tried not to watch. He really was a hateful man, pumping her for information and then cutting her off. She would do well to remember that he was no friend to anyone there. For a brief time she had forgotten that but it would not happen again.

"When the paperwork comes through, I'll release it to you," she clipped.

"Thank you."

"You're welcome."

Her chin was angled up and sparks still flashed in her eyes.

Christian sighed. It was hard to keep his distance when she looked like that. He took a step forward.

She tried to back away then realized she was trapped, her hips pressed against the row of files.

"That's what happens to damsels," he murmured, smiling. "They find themselves in distress."

"Do you realize that makes you the dragon? No one else is here."

He laughed and the sound vibrated along Sonya's nerve endings. She looked quickly away, her heart starting a rapid tattoo, her senses coming to instantaneous life.

At that moment Barbara...dear, sweet, efficient Barbara...came around the corner and stopped practically in midstride. "Oh!" she cried, surprised...and immediately broke Sonya's near paralytic state. Taking advantage of Christian's distraction,

Sonya pushed the drawer closed and slipped to freedom.

Barbara's almond-shaped eyes were large. "I thought I heard voices." She had been told that Sonya was on special assignment, but she had been given no information about the reappearance of the collection.

"We're just leaving," Sonya said, and turned away, hoping that Christian would follow. He did, and so did Barbara.

In the more open area of the work room, Sonya turned to her assistant and asked, "Did the San Diego shipment arrive on time?"

"Yes. On Tuesday."

"And was everything properly packed this time?"

"Yes. No breakage."

"What about the Conner exhibit? Has it left the museum yet?"

"I sent it off yesterday."

Sonya gave a tight smile. "Good."

Barbara mistook her taut feeling for irritation and hurried to explain, "If you've heard what Ted's been saying, it's none of my doing, Sonya. I don't want your job. He's using me to get at you and I don't like it any more than you do."

"I never thought . . ."

"But you wondered. I just wanted you to know. We've always worked well together. I don't want that to change."

"Nothing will change," Sonya assured her, and as she said the words, she knew she had little faith in them. Somehow she had the feeling that *everything* would change and that it was going to happen soon.

Barbara looked relieved. She glanced at Christian, smiled and excused herself.

Sonya watched her move away. It wasn't easy to be witness to the fact that you could easily be replaced. But if anyone did replace her, she hoped it would be Barbara. She was as nice as she was capable.

She felt Christian's eyes and darted him a glance. "Is something wrong?"

He smiled. "Not a thing."

"Then quit looking at me like that."

"I like to look at you."

Sonya sighed. "Shouldn't we be doing something?"

"I got the feeling a few minutes ago that you wanted to get away from me."

"I'm talking about hunting for the thief."

"So you *want* to do that now?"

She made an impatient gesture. "I thought that's what this whole idea was about? If you've changed your mind, I'd appreciate your letting me know. You just heard again that my job is threatened. If this is some kind of game to you, let me out of it!"

"It's not a game."

"Then let's get on with it! Anyway, the quicker you're satisfied that you've either found the person responsible or that you're not going to find the person, the quicker my life can get back to normal."

"And be orderly."

"Yes."

"And serious."

"Yes."

"And boring?"

"No!"

He laughed and swinging an arm round her shoulders, swept her up the stairs with him. He was still laughing as they stepped into the museum. Several museum goers, startled by the disruption to their quiet, cast disapproving stares, which caused Christian to laugh all the harder.

THE NOTE WAS NOT NOTICEABLE at first. Both had taken their seats in the car—Christian had even started the engine—before he saw the folded paper tucked carefully beneath the driver's side wiper blade.

He shifted gears into neutral and stepped out to retrieve it. Then settling back into the car again he murmured, "At least it's not a parking ticket. Wrong color."

Sonya said nothing.

He opened the paper, read it and smiled before handing it to her.

Sonya accepted it curiously, and as she scanned the contents, her eyes widened with each succinctly pasted word.

Leave well enough alone. Don't make me have to tell you again!

"You find this amusing?" she challenged, looking back at him.

"It means we're hitting a nerve."

"An unbalanced nerve, it seems."

"Probably not. Someone doesn't want us poking into the past. That, to me, means we're getting close."

"So we're going to keep on?"

"Of course."

"But the note—"

"Is just a note." He put the car in gear.

Somehow Sonya didn't think it was quite as simple as that.

Before driving away from the curb, Christjan took the paper from her hand and slipped it into his breast pocket. "Evidence," he explained. "For when we both end up dead."

Her eyes grew larger.

His white teeth flashed. "I'm teasing!"

Sonya would not be teased, not about that. She turned to look out the window and didn't turn back until they started to leave the city by way of the Golden Gate.

"I suppose you have a destination in mind?" she asked.

"Of course."

"Would you mind telling me what it is?"

"You're interested again?"

Sonya firmed her jaw. "If I'm going to be killed for it . . . yes, I'd like to know."

He shook his head. "You're a stubborn person."

"Very," she agreed.

He darted her an approving glance, then said, "We're driving to Muir Woods. There's someone there we want to see."

"Who, may I ask?"

"You may. His name is Sam Peterson. He was a police detective assigned to the case. He's retired now and manages the concession stand at the park."

"How did you find him?"

"I have my ways."

Sonya gazed out over the bay. A multitude of sailboats were taking advantage of the pretty day, Alcatraz Island was a distant reminder of some men's fate, and the Bay Bridge wove its long, graceful path from the city to Treasure Island to the East Bay. Berkeley, nestled between the water and a building set of hills, looked innocent and inviting. In the four years since moving to the area, she had never tired of its natural beauty.

Shortly they were turning onto a narrow road where the smell of eucalyptus leaves permeated the air. Sharp hairpin turns soon had Sonya clinging to her seat, trying not to rest too freely on Christian's shoulder on one side and the door on the other.

He seemed to enjoy everything about the drive.

WHEN THEY ARRIVED, Sonya stepped from the car. Muir Woods could be counted among her most favorite places on earth. Though not all that widely traveled, she could not imagine another habitat more beautiful. It had to be what the forest primeval was like all those centuries ago when the planet was newly born and man had yet to begin to leave his mark. Giant redwoods thrust into the sky, their lacy leaves making a canopy over gigantic ferns and rich, rich loam. A swiftly moving stream played alongside the walkway. Moisture seemed suspended in the air here, dripping patiently from leaf to leaf. Sonya slipped on her jacket, glad for the warmth.

Christian walked at her side, past row after row of cars. Sonya was not the only one to think the preserve special. People came from around the world to witness it.

Near the front entrance, a volunteer was handing out information sheets, as a ranger was gathering a group of visitors for a special tour.

The two of them slipped past. They were here on business, not pleasure, although pleasure wasn't something that could be avoided.

The greatness of the place was magnified by its deep silence. People talked, but the sound seemed to be absorbed. In no way did one human being intrude on another.

They followed the path a short distance to the concession stand. Sonya wasn't surprised that Christian needed no directions. He was probably as familiar with the layout as she was.

As he held the door open, his gaze caught hers. Against the lush green backdrop, his handsome features and reckless air seemed magnified. This was more his element than hers. She loved it, but he *lived* it. She was far too timid a soul even to think of doing some of the things she was sure that he had done. She put on a good show of being determined, but underneath she knew that she hesitated when he did not.

Sliding her gaze away, she pretended to negotiate carefully the step up into the small building. Once inside, the aroma of freshly brewed coffee enveloped them.

One third of the building was a gift shop stocked with every sort of redwood souvenir imaginable, from unbelievably tiny seeds in containers to giant redwood carvings. The rest was comprised of the snack bar and tables.

Christian collected a tray and moved down the line. "Hot dog?" he asked Sonya. "Mustard? A Coke?"

"Sprite," she corrected, for the first time disagreeing.

He flashed a smile. "Diet?"

Sonya threw caution to the wind. "No. Straight."

The smile he gave was appreciative.

Christian brought the tray to the table Sonya had picked out, one closest to the glass wall in order to enjoy the beautiful view. In virtual silence they ate their simple meal.

As they were finishing, a man approached. Very fit for a person in his sixties, he could put most younger men to shame. His biceps were honed, his stomach hard and flat. His hair was a closely cropped mixture of ash and silver.

Christian dispatched with the introductions quickly and the man took a seat.

"It's going to get crowded later, so let's not waste time. You said you wanted to know something about the museum theft that happened when I was on the force. What do you want to know?"

"Well, who did it, actually," Christian replied.

The man's gaze narrowed. "Want to explain that?"

"We know who everyone *said* did it. What we want to know is who really did it."

"What makes you think I have any idea?"

"I've dealt with professionals like you before. I know you usually form an opinion. What's yours?"

"I might have one, but that and a nickel will get you a stick of gum."

"I'll chance it."

The man's eyes had remained narrow. "Why are you sticking your neck out? Those old pieces of junk are bad luck."

"I don't believe in luck."

"Well, I do, and for good reason. I'm still here, alive and kicking, when I shouldn't be. I'm carrying around two fairly large pieces of metal. One from the war. Another from the police force. I call that luck."

Christian nodded. "I would, too."

The man gave Sonya an aggressive look. "How do you fit into this?"

She lifted her chin. She certainly wasn't along as decoration. "I work at the museum. I'm senior registrar there."

He frowned, concentrated, then said, "Amanda Bradley. She was the registrar at the time of the theft."

Sonya nodded. "She was registrar until about ten years ago."

"What happened to her? She was a nice lady. Gruff but nice."

"She died."

"See? Bad luck."

"At eighty-five."

"She should have made eighty-six."

When Sam Peterson grinned, his face changed from bulldog intensity to puckish amusement. He relaxed for the first time since sitting down with them. "I'm sorry. Sometimes I forget I'm retired." He took a sip of the orange-colored drink he had brought with him. "I don't know very much more to tell you than what's already on record. Tomas Delia was arrested, then he was released because we lacked proper evidence. That seemed to be the end of it."

"Why was that the end of it?" Christian probed. "Why didn't the investigation continue?"

"Oh, it did. I tried to keep it alive. But as time went by, so many other things were happening—murders, kidnappings, rapes—that it got pushed to a back burner."

"It was your case entirely?"

"Me and my partner's."

"Is your partner..."

"He died a couple of years ago."

Christian went back to his original question. "What opinion did you draw? Did you think Delia did it?"

"Hell, no."

"Why not?"

"He was just this poor immigrant, trying to get along, and we pounced on him."

"To have someone you could say did it?"

Peterson studied his hands. "I'm not exactly proud of that. I knew he didn't do it, my partner knew he didn't do it. But when we were told to come up with someone or else...we came up with him. He was a likely suspect. He'd just lost another job due to some kind of misunderstanding and he'd had the most recent contact with the goods."

"When he took the exhibit to the railway station," Sonya supplied.

Peterson nodded. "He swore the boxes had been tampered with before they came into his possession. No one believed him . . . at least, no one *wanted* to believe him."

"I have reason to think that someone from inside the museum was responsible," Christian said.

A quick return to the intense bulldog. "What reason?"

Sonya caught Christian's eye. He responded by winking.

"I can't reveal my source."

"You sound like a newsman," Peterson said disgustedly.

"Usually I'm accused of being a cop."

The man smiled, relaxing again. "Two scourges on society. At least, that's the way some people feel . . . until they need a cop."

"Didn't you wonder about that yourself? Check into it a bit."

"Yes, but I couldn't get anywhere with it. People were closed up tighter than a drum."

Christian reached into his pocket and withdrew the folded note. He scooted it across the table. "This was on my car right before we came here."

The man read it and said, "I still have some connections on the force. Want me to get a run-through done?"

"It wouldn't hurt."

"Are you taking this as a threat?"

"No, a compliment."

The ex-policeman nodded. "You might be right."

Christian glanced at Sonya and stood up. "We'll be in touch."

"Sorry I couldn't help you more. Call me in a couple of days. I might have something for you by then."

Christian nodded.

As they started out the door, Sam Peterson's voice followed, "You might want to watch your back a little. It never hurts to be careful. Just in case."

THE FOREST REMAINED bathed in silence. So many years of growth, hundreds for each tree. Some had been fully mature when the New World was discovered.

"Do you think he was serious?" Sonya asked. The threatening note had bothered her, but being in a place where life was telescoped so minutely made her appreciate her relatively shorter life span even more.

"About us watching our backs?"

"Yes."

"I wouldn't think it would hurt, but then, it never hurts. Half of any battle is being prepared."

"You learned that from your pirate ancestor?"

"I learned it from my father...one time when we were on safari and a lion almost ate me for lunch."

Totally unexpected. He was always doing that...coming out with things that disconcerted her.

"Well, are you going to tell me more?" she demanded.

"About the lion?"

"I didn't mean your father."

"I'll tell you about both."

He took her arm and she knew that after today she would never think of these woods again without associating them with Christian and his hungry lion.

Chapter Eight

Christian fought his way through layers of sleep. Someone was calling his name, but he was too muzzy to tell if the person was a dream or reality. His shoulder was being abused, though, so he struggled to sit up, hoping to make the abuse stop.

He opened a bleary eye and the face of the youngest of his sisters came into focus. She was looking at him in exasperation while shaking his shoulder once again.

"Stop that!" he grumbled, pushing her hand away. "Are you trying to break it?"

His sister's hair was a dark cloud around her face. Full and vibrant, it curled in a great mass over her shoulders. Her features were much like Christian's—drawn with a master's touch. Her eyes were a different color, though, as black as the night that waited past the pool of light cast by his bedside lamp.

"What a wonderful greeting, and with me flying halfway around the world to see you."

"Couldn't you have waited to say hello until morning?"

"It's afternoon to me, London time."

Christian glanced at the bedside clock. "It's barely six!"

"I thought you liked to rise early."

"Not this early."

Letitia giggled. "You look like a disturbed bear. No wonder you're still single. One look at you in your unadulterated state and you'd frighten the poor girl away."

Christian folded his pillow behind his back, propping it against the headboard. "You're talking to your brother, remember? I've seen you in some pretty awful states yourself. If you tell, I tell."

A shadow passed over her beautiful face. "You have no one to tell now."

Christian cursed his thoughtlessness. "You and Misha are still apart?"

"We're about as apart as any two people can be. It got to be that way even when we were in the same room."

"You okay?" he asked.

"I thought I loved him, Chris. And maybe I still do, because whenever I think of him, it hurts. But *he* doesn't think I love him. He says I only love myself." After a miserable pause she whispered, "I don't want that to be true."

"It's not true."

"But the same thing has happened to so many Townsends! It's like a curse or something. Think back. None of our family has ever been very lucky in love. Something always seems to happen, to get in the way. I don't understand how Mom and Dad stayed together all these years. They're the exception to the rule."

"That shows it's not a curse. Curses don't skip people."

"The Townsend curse could."

"So now it has a name?"

"I named it."

"Very original."

A tiny smile played at her lips before being banished. She motioned to him. "Look at you. You're not exactly bursting with domestic bliss. Neither is Gillian or Odette." She shook her head. "No, something has to be wrong with us. We can't relate to people. It's a failing."

Christian moved against his pillow. This wasn't what he wanted to hear right now. He had had enough trouble getting to sleep last night with thoughts of Sonya Douglas pestering him to distraction. And now Letitia was descending on him with her doom and gloom.

"We're perfectly ordinary people," he assured. "Nothing more, nothing less."

"Perfectly ordinary people don't live like we do. Come on, Chris. Gillian with her camels and ostriches and llamas. Odette and her crazy films. Mom and Dad . . . Well, Mom and Dad being the way they are. And you? You scoot from one part of the globe to another, your finger in all sorts of pies, none of which could be considered ordinary."

"I dabble in the sciences," Christian defended. "Nothing wrong with that."

"You live out other men's dreams!"

"I get things done that wouldn't be done otherwise."

"I'm not saying you don't! I'm just telling you that you're different. We all are! And we pay for that difference in ways other people don't."

"So should we try a mass suicide?"

Letitia made a disgusted sound. "You haven't been listening. I'm trying to make an important point and you couldn't care less. That's another thing about this family, we're all pigheaded!"

"Speak for yourself, dear sister. *I* am a veritable font of sensitivity."

Letitia stared at him blankly before starting to laugh. "Single-minded, is more like it. What have you found out about Uncle's collection?"

"Not much, except that it's all together and in fine shape."

"Do you have any ideas about who did it yet?"

"Are you planning to help?"

"No, I'm going to shop, be with some friends . . . in general, lick my wounds while I lie low for a while. I didn't think you'd mind if I shared the house since I plan to stay mostly in my own rooms."

"Not in the least."

She leaned forward to kiss his stubble-roughened cheek. "Have I ever told you you're my favorite brother?"

"A few times."

"Good. I might do it a few more. Now, go back to sleep. Dream sweet dreams. And don't worry about what I said. Sometimes I just run off at the mouth.

Misha always said—'' She stopped. "To hell with what Misha said! He's not part of my life anymore."

"Good for you!"

"But I do still think I love him."

"You'll get over it if you're meant to."

Letitia gave him a considering look. "Something about you is different."

"I've stopped parting my hair on the wrong side." He grinned.

"You've never parted your hair on the side. No, it's something else. Something I can't yet—"

He yawned. "If you keep talking, it will be light and I'll never get back to sleep."

She ruffled his hair as she had done when they were children, a time when the three years that separated them seemed much greater. "You want me to tuck you in?" she teased.

"That won't be necessary, thank you."

"Sleep tight, then...and don't let the bed bugs bite. Remember that? Mom and Dad used to say it all the time when we were little."

Christian remembered. He also remembered using the phrase on a much more recent occasion, which instantly had the effect of obliterating any further hope of rest. Because when thoughts of Sonya Douglas entered his mind, *rest* wasn't the word that described his emotional state.

SONYA WAS WALKING PAST the security station, moving from one area of the museum to another, when Julia, the guard on duty, motioned for her to stop.

"Who *is* that man I've seen you with lately? The one I called you about the other day? Every time he comes into the museum, he remembers me. He smiles and waves. If I weren't a married woman who loves her husband, I think I'd try to get something going in that direction. He is some *prime* cut of meat."

Sonya had always liked Julia who was good at her job and friendly in the bargain. But when she described Christian in such a manner, Sonya cringed. It was as repulsive to her to hear a man referred to without respect as it was for a woman to be treated the same way. Especially Christian. They didn't always get along. In fact, she'd just as soon he leave the city right this minute and disappear to his usual haunts. But she did sense that he didn't trade on his good looks. There was more to him than that. He was complicated, multidimensional, and deserved respect.

Her voice was stiff as she answered, "He's a friend of mine."

Julia didn't get the hint. "A good friend?"

"Good enough," she continued the lie.

"You mean you and he are—"

"I mean nothing. We're friends. Period."

"If that's what you say."

"That's exactly what I say."

"Well, excuse me. I didn't mean to offend."

Sonya saw the affront the other woman had suffered. She sighed and answered more affably, "You didn't offend. Ah...has he been here yet today?"

Julia unbent a degree. "Not yet."

"If he comes in during the next few minutes, will you tell him I'm on an errand and won't be long?"

"Certainly."

Sonya nodded and continued on her way. This morning, at first light, she had awakened to the idea that she had seen the typeface used in the warning note before. The bits and pieces of lettering were both unique and familiar and she was sure that she had seen it in the gift shop.

Entering the small room, she went directly to the brochures that advertised upcoming showings and began to look through them. Soon she found what she was after. The print on the circular extolling an upcoming showing of pre-Columbian art was exactly the same. It had the same double-sided lettering, the same type of scroll, even the background color and color of print was the same. The person who had placed the note on the car had to have taken the lettering from a brochure like this one. The coincidence was too close for doubt.

Sonya slid a copy of the brochure into her pocket.

WAITING AT THE FRONT DESK, Christian leaned casually against its maple surface, watching two volunteers fill giant terra-cotta vases at the entrance of the museum with a striking array of dried flowers and leaves. He glanced over, saw Sonya and smiled.

His rakish charm jolted Sonya even at a distance. She paused, then forced herself to go forward to meet him.

"Good morning," he greeted, a lazy warmth to his words. "I was told to wait here and you'd turn up."

Sonya nodded. "I left word."

He straightened. "That was considerate."

She glanced at the progress of the dried arrangements and complimented the workers when first one, then the other, looked across at her.

Christian watched her silently, his gaze fastened on her profile. "I received a call about an hour ago."

"Oh?" She turned back to him. The color of her eyes was so very different from his sister's. Where Letitia's were night dark and mysterious, Sonya's were a rich, warm chocolate that were most comfortable when receptive. At present, though, they were guarded.

"Mrs. Richards, the librarian. Her son gave his permission for us to go through his father's papers. Only we're not to take anything or make any copies."

"Something we can live with."

"Easily. Are you ready?"

"We're going now?"

"From the way she talked, there are a number of boxes. We might as well get started."

A NUMBER OF BOXES was an understatement. Ralph Richards must have never thrown anything away.

The librarian smiled serenely at their looks of dismay. "I did tell you there was a garage full."

Christian gazed at the product of one man's lifetime. "Would they be filed in any particular order?"

"I doubt it. Ralph never liked to put things where another person would think to look for them. He had his own system. His retirement dream was to gather everything up and make a book out of the better parts. He never got to do that, though. I was hoping that Donald would, but he's always so busy."

"Do you have any suggestions as to where we should start?"

"Oh, my, no. Just anywhere."

Two hours later Sonya and Christian had examined the contents of four boxes. Ralph Richard's filing system was a shotgun affair with notes on one subject sprinkled liberally from one box to another. Dates seemed to have no order. Notes from the beginning of his career were mingled with notes from close to the end.

Christian dropped a yellow pad filled with the now-familiar scratching back into place. "Did I mention something about Sanskrit before?"

Sonya was frowning at a scrap of paper, trying to make out the highly-personalized shorthand. She was getting much better at deciphering it. "It's very logical. He didn't change his method. The words are abbreviated the same way each time. It's just hard to read at first."

"We're going to go blind."

"No, we're not."

He dug out another packet of notes. "Slave driver."

Sonya grinned.

Another hour passed before Christian stood up. "That's it. I can't handle any more. We can come back tomorrow and the next day, but no more for now."

Sonya rubbed her eyes. History had always been one of her favorite subjects and this was history unfolding right before her eyes. It jumped from one time period to the next, from one topic to another, unlike any textbook she had ever studied, but it was far more interesting and alive. The notes were more like bits of gossip: how someone had looked, what they wore, whether Ralph thought they were trying to evade a question and why. He had the soul of a novelist and she regretted that he had never been given the chance to translate his thoughts into a book. It might have been a best-seller. She marked her place by tilting a yellowed sheet on edge then stood up without protest.

Christian smiled understanding when she swayed slightly. "I've been accused of being single-minded, but I think you've got a worse case of it than I do. You're actually enjoying this."

"It is rather fascinating."

Christian's eyes were warm with admiration. "I really do appreciate your help."

"What if it's all for nothing? What if we never find anything to connect anyone to the theft?"

"You mean here?"

"Anywhere."

"Then I'll know that I've done my best—that we've done *our* best."

"You think your uncle would be satisfied with that?"

"I've told you. I'm not doing this for my uncle. I'm doing it for me."

"You said you were here thirty years ago. You couldn't have been very old."

"I was seven."

"Old enough to remember." When he made no comment, she said, "You really loved your uncle, didn't you?"

"He was a special man."

Flora Richards stepped into the garage, carrying a tray filled with cups, saucers, and a coffee server. "I thought you might be getting tired." She glanced at the open boxes. "Oh, you've made a nice start."

Christian held the tray while she found a place for it. The workbench ended up serving as a table.

"SUCH NICE YOUNG PEOPLE," Mrs. Richards observed later while collecting the used cups. "Are you engaged?"

Sonya pretended not to have heard. Thankfully, she had been studying an old quilting frame strapped to the ceiling of the garage and kept her gaze firmly fixed on it.

Christian had no such luck, but, as usual, he was ready with a quick reply. "The lady won't have me," he said sadly.

Mrs. Richards immediately directed a shocked look at Sonya, one she couldn't ignore. Her color heightened as the older woman asked, "My dear, why ever not?"

Sonya felt Christian's laughing gaze, but she refused to be drawn to look at him. The sneaky bastard. "Because he thinks too much of himself," she explained. "And he likes to order me around."

"He's just trying to show you how much he cares."

"He has shocking table manners. He was on his best behavior today, but I've seen him really shoveling it in and letting food drip on his shirt in his hurry."

The woman's gaze swung back to Christian.

"She exaggerates," he explained.

Now Flora Richards didn't know who to believe. Neither did she know what to say. So she cleared her throat, giving a tiny, uncomfortable, "Ah-hem."

When Christian started to laugh, there was something so very appealing about him. Sonya retained her outward objectivity only with great difficulty.

"We're putting you on, Mrs. Richards," Christian said. "Sonya and I are merely friends."

The woman accepted his explanation, then smugly said, "But friendships often turn into something more. I do so hope yours does. You make such a striking couple."

After helping the woman clear up, Sonya couldn't wait to get to the car. She flopped into her seat and glowered straight ahead.

Christian wisely said nothing until after they had pulled away from the curb. "You're angry with me?"

"Oh, a little," she said tightly.

"I thought her mistake was amusing."

"I know. That's why I'm angry."

"You need to loosen up, Sonya. You did for a minute. I almost fell over when you said I dribbled."

Sonya tapped her fingers on the dash as her mind filled in a picture of the debonair Christian dribbling. In spite of her intention not to, she began to smile.

"Come on," he said. "Let it happen. You did earlier and the earth didn't stop."

"I did what?" She was still fighting it.

"You smiled. All on your own. Without even thinking about it."

"I did not."

"Did too."

The second smile won out. His goading was powerful, especially combined with the teasing mischief in his eyes.

Again, wisely, he made no comment.

A short time later he said, "I've got to be somewhere for a couple of hours. Nothing to do with the collection. So I'll pick you up at about four? Is that okay? I thought we'd pay Mrs. Delia another call. See if she's willing now to shed a little more light."

"All right." For some reason, Sonya felt let down.

Christian sent her a quick look from the corner of his eye. Did she sound disappointed? The idea intrigued him.

WHILE SHE WAS TRAMPING UP the long series of steps to the museum's back door, David was returning, as well. He hesitated before calling out to her, she looked so distracted. They arrived at the door at the same time. Sonya started when she discovered that she was not alone.

"You look tired again." David's half smile was deprecating.

Again his comment irritated her. "I know you're concerned for me, but David, please, don't keep telling me how bad I look. It throws any confidence I might be able to muster right out the window."

"I'm sorry. I didn't mean..."

Conscious of his feelings, she quickly recanted, "No, please. It's me. I'm the one who's sorry. It's just—"

When she didn't continue, he opened the door for her and said, "It's that Townsend man, isn't it? He's upsetting you. I'll have a word with Ted. He can't continue to make you do this, not when it's detrimental to your health. I'll tell him that.''

Sonya was surprised by David's evolution from meek and mild to meek and not so mild. "No. It's all right. I don't want you to speak to him. I don't want to give him any excuse.''

"But it's not fair!''

"I'm not being hurt. If I were, I'd stop it myself.''

"I still don't like it.''

Sonya paused at the door leading to the lower level. "Not many people have friends as loyal as you. I appreciate that, David, but I can take care of myself. I've been doing it for a number of years and plan to for a number more. You don't have to worry.''

"Everyone needs to be taken care of sometime.''

"But only if they want to be. Otherwise, the person trying to impose that care becomes as irritating as the person who ignores them completely. Possibly even more so.''

"You're telling me to butt out, aren't you?''

Sonya smiled wryly. "Well, not exactly in those words.''

David sighed. "I don't want to see you get hurt, Sonya.''

"I won't. Trust me.''

"It's not that . . .''

Sonya had had enough. She gave his arm a reassuring squeeze and said, "I've got to go. Christian and I have another appointment later this afternoon, and I have to get lunch and see to a couple of things. Can we talk more later?''

David dipped his head. "Sure. Later."

Sonya's conscience pricked as she let the door close behind her, but she couldn't deal with anything else at that moment. She needed to hole up in her office and try to collect herself. When the rest of the day involved Christian Townsend, heaven only knew what would happen, and possibly even the saints weren't fully apprised.

CHRISTIAN HAD DIFFICULTY concentrating on what his sister was saying as they lunched at her favorite San Francisco restaurant.

Letitia had perked up considerably, either that or she was putting on a good act. She was bright and laughing and accepting her friends' greetings with alacrity.

At the end of the meal, she sat back and said, "I haven't enjoyed myself like this in ages. Thank you, Christian. This was a wonderful idea."

"You were the one who wanted to come here."

"But you agreed. I do so hate eating at restaurants alone. People look at you as if you have two heads or as if they expect that any moment you're going to do something wildly wicked to entertain them. You can feel their beady little eyes boring into you."

"You have a wild imagination."

She grinned. "Comes in handy in my line of work, all those striking designs that people seem to like so much. Don't disparage it."

"Oh, I wouldn't dream of it. Anything that keeps you occupied so you're not getting into trouble."

"Oh! You have a nerve. You caused a lot more trouble growing up than I did."

"But you got caught more."

"Only because you were sneakier . . . and could run faster."

"Guilty as charged, dear sister."

"That's not necessarily something to brag about."

"I prefer *cleverer*."

"I omitted that on purpose."

"I noticed."

Christian glanced at his watch.

"That's the hundredth time you've done that," Letitia complained. "Am I boring you? Because if I am, you don't have to stay."

Christian smiled. "You could never be boring. No, it's that I have to be somewhere at four."

"Where?" she immediately demanded.

"To talk to someone about the theft."

"May I come along?"

"I thought you weren't interested."

"I'm interested. I just don't want to get tied down."

Christian settled his napkin on the table. "This time I'm afraid you're out of luck. I've already made arrangements with someone else."

"Who?"

"Someone from the museum."

"Is it a he or a she?"

"A she."

"Tell her she can't come."

Christian was amused by Letitia's imperiousness. "No."

His sister's eyes narrowed. "Do I detect something else in that answer? Exactly how stunning is she?"

"Not really very stunning at all."

"Do clocks stop when she walks by?"

Christian laughed. "No."

"I'm coming along to meet her."

"No, you can't. My car only holds two."

"I think there's something you don't want me to know. Remember, I'm older than you. I know all your tricks."

"That's only because you taught them to me."

"Don't try to change the subject. I want to meet her."

"Why?"

"To give my approval."

"I'm not marrying her, only taking her to a meeting."

"Meetings can be dangerous. That's where I met Misha."

"It's not the same thing, I assure you."

"So you're not interested in her. Is she married or something?"

"No."

"Then?"

He groaned. "You're worse than Mother. When you want to know something, you don't give up."

"I'll take that as a compliment. All right. This time I'll let you get away with it, on the condition that you bring her by the house sometime. I want to meet the woman who has you all atwitter."

"I'm not atwitter."

Letitia stood up. "Indulge me," she cooed.

Christian sighed. He knew he was fighting a losing battle. When any of his sisters dug their heels in, that was the end of it until they got what they wanted. He thought of Sonya and Letitia together. He wondered how the combination would mix.

Chapter Nine

The wrought-iron security gate remained firmly in place in front of the entrance to the Delia house. There was no welcoming hand to unlatch it, no full opening of the door. Instead, through a six-inch crack, Theresa Delia looked out at them, the change in her demeanor unsettling.

Christian glanced at Sonya before saying, "Mrs. Delia? We apologize for dropping by like this, but if you could give us a few minutes more of your time—"

There was no friendliness in the older woman's expression. "Go away. I do not wish to see you."

Christian frowned. "But you said . . ."

"I say many things and regret them." She started to close the door.

Christian reached through the bars to hold the door steady. "Another time, then. Tomorrow?"

"I have told you everything I have to say."

Sonya stepped closer. "What are you afraid of, Mrs. Delia?"

"I am afraid of nothing except God."

"Then why not talk to us? We're trying to help your husband, not hurt him."

The woman threw Sonya a deprecating look. "What do you know of hurt? It was your museum that doubted him, your museum that put him in jail, your museum that caused my family—" She broke off, biting her lip to halt the flow of words.

Sonya's voice softened. "Please let us help you."

The woman's gaze wavered but that weakness was quickly covered. She pushed against the door, wordlessly ordering Christian to release it.

"Has someone threatened you, Mrs. Delia?" Christian asked. "Because if they have . . ."

"I am afraid of no one. Only God, as I say. I do not wish to speak with you again. Leave me alone."

She pushed the door with greater strength and Christian let go. It closed with an unsatisfactory thump.

THEY WALKED IN SILENCE to the car. Several people waved at Christian and he waved casually in return.

Sonya was frowning as he slid into the seat beside her. "That woman was afraid," she said firmly, digging in her purse for the brochure she had collected earlier. "I've found something interesting. It looks like a match to the lettering of our warning note."

He studied the paper, turning it to see the museum's insignia printed on the front. His gaze jumped to hers, speculative.

"That doesn't mean a thing. There are about a thousand like this in the gift shop. It's one of our ways of advertising."

"So anyone could have picked one up and used it."
She nodded.

He rested his hands on the steering wheel. "We should be hearing from Sam Peterson soon. Maybe then we'll have more of a clue."

"Why do you think someone doesn't want us to learn the truth about the past? Do you think they did it? Or that they know who did and are trying to shield either them or their memory?"

Christian started the car. "At this point, one guess is as good as another." They swung into traffic.

"But who would involve Mrs. Delia? The threat must have been pretty strong to make her behave as she did."

"She's an old woman. Possibly we've made her remember too much and she's not happy with the pain."

"No, she's been threatened and she's taking it seriously."

Sonya lapsed into silence. None of it made sense, but then, so far, very little of the entire affair had. Why would someone steal the exhibit all those years before and then hide it inside the museum? Had the thief meant to come get it later and been unable to? Could this merely be a wild-goose chase after someone who had been dead for years? Yet if that was the case, why was Mrs. Delia acting so cautiously? And why the threatening note?

Christian was as suspicious as Sonya. But he had learned long ago not to jump headfirst into a pool that he was unfamiliar with. They would give it a little more time. He hadn't expected the process to be easy.

OPEN YOUR DOOR
TO HARLEQUIN

Send us this bouquet

AND WE'LL SEND YOU
4 HARLEQUIN
AMERICAN ROMANCE
NOVELS

FREE
PLUS TWO FREE GIFTS

NOW THAT THE DOOR IS OPEN...
Peel off the bouquet and send it on the postpaid order card to receive:

4 FREE BOOKS
from

HARLEQUIN
American Romance®

An attractive 20k gold electroplated chain FREE! And a mystery gift as an EXTRA BONUS!

PLUS

FREE HOME DELIVERY!

Once you receive your 4 FREE books and gifts, you'll be able to open your door to more great romance reading month after month. Enjoy the convenience of previewing 4 brand-new books every month delivered right to your home months before they appear in stores. Each book is yours for the low member-only price of $2.74* — that's 21 cents off the retail cover price — with no additional charges for home delivery.

SPECIAL EXTRAS — FREE!

You'll also receive the "Heart to Heart" Newsletter FREE with every book shipment. Every issue is filled with interviews, news about upcoming books and more! And as a valued reader, we'll be sending you additional free gifts from time to time — as a token of our appreciation.

NO-RISK GUARANTEE!

- There's no obligation to buy — and the free books and gifts are yours to keep forever.
- You pay the low members' only price and receive books months before they appear in stores.
- You may cancel at any time, for any reason, just by sending us a note or a shipping statement marked "cancel" or by returning any shipment of books to us at our cost. Either way the free books and gifts are yours to keep!

RETURN THE POSTPAID ORDER CARD TODAY AND OPEN YOUR DOOR TO THESE 4 EXCITING LOVE-FILLED NOVELS. THEY ARE YOURS ABSOLUTELY FREE ALONG WITH YOUR 20k GOLD ELECTROPLATED CHAIN AND MYSTERY GIFT.

*Terms and prices subject to change without notice.
 Sales tax applicable in NY and Iowa.
© 1989 Harlequin Enterprises Ltd.

FREE! 20k GOLD ELECTROPLATED CHAIN!

You'll love this 20k gold electroplated chain! The necklace is finely crafted with 160 double-soldered links and is electroplate finished in genuine 20k gold. It's nearly ⅛" wide, fully 20" long — and has the look and feel of the real thing. "Glamorous" is the perfect word for it, and it is yours free with this offer!

HARLEQUIN READER SERVICE
901 FUHRMANN BLVD
PO BOX 1867
BUFFALO NY 14240-9952

Place the
Bouquet
here →

Yes! I have attached the bouquet above. Please rush me my four Harlequin AMERICAN ROMANCE® novels along with my FREE 20k Electroplated Gold Chain and mystery gift as explained on the opposite page. I understand that accepting these books and gifts places me under no obligation ever to buy any books. I may cancel at any time for any reason, and the free books and gifts will be mine to keep!

154 CIH NBJC
(U-H-A-03/90)

Name _____

Address _____ Apt. _____

City _____ State _____

Zip _____

Offer limited to one per household and not valid for present Harlequin American Romance subscribers. Terms and prices subject to change without notice. Orders subject to approval.

© 1989 Harlequin Enterprises Ltd.

PRINTED IN U.S.A.

Take this beautiful
20k GOLD
ELECTROPLATED CHAIN
with your 4 FREE BOOKS
PLUS A MYSTERY GIFT
If offer card is missing, write to: Harlequin Reader Service,
901 Fuhrmann Blvd., P.O. Box 1867, Buffalo, NY 14269-1867.

PLACE THE BOOKLET ON THIS SIDE FIRST. THEN FOLD

NO POSTAGE
NECESSARY
IF MAILED
IN THE
UNITED STATES

BUSINESS REPLY CARD

First Class   Permit No. 717   Buffalo, NY

Postage will be paid by addressee

HARLEQUIN READER SERVICE
901 FUHRMANN BLVD
PO BOX 1867
BUFFALO NY 14240-9952

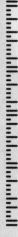

CHRISTIAN HELD the tiny green bottle to the light. It seemed that for most of his life he had had a special affinity to its curving delicacy. He remembered with perfect clarity his first encounter with the mysterious flash of green. He had tried repeatedly that first summer to make the fire reappear, but no matter what he did, it would not come. Eventually, in frustration, he had confided the occurrence to his uncle.

"The light only comes at special times, my Christian," Dominic had replied. "And to special people. You are one of them."

Christian remembered asking if his uncle had ever seen it. With a beautiful smile, his uncle had nodded.

The bottle felt good in his hands again. Substantial, not a memory. It was as if both he and it had come home.

The other pieces of the collection were not nearly so dear to him as this one small object. He knew his uncle had felt the same way. When it had been stolen along with the rest, his uncle had mourned for it with greater intensity.

The bottle was magic or at least, at six, he had thought that. But he had been a child then and his uncle had been indulgent . . . and full of stories.

With regret, Christian returned the bottle to the tray.

"Is something wrong?" Sonya asked, looking up from the paperwork that would release the collection to him.

Christian shook his head.

"Does the bottle have a crack?"

"No, it's fine."

A thoughtful look settled on her face, then slowly she asked, "Is there something special about that particular piece?"

"Why do you ask?"

"I'm curious. You go directly to it each time."

Had there been an odd hesitancy in her voice? "My uncle was visiting at a villa outside Florence when he was a young man. He had a passion for archaeology, and since an area on the outskirts of the villa grounds had been damaged by an earthquake hundreds of years before, he asked for permission to search through the rubble. For weeks he came up with nothing, then when he was about to give up, he found these." He indicated the collection. "That's why they were so special to him. It was his first discovery."

"I've seen him referred to as Professor Townsend. He was a teacher?"

"Not formally. He preferred to do rather than tell. But he was quite respected because he was on the vanguard of archaeology as a modern science. Before, people pretty much ruined ancient sites trying to get to the valuable objects. They ignored everything else, or worse, deliberately destroyed it. Because of ignorance? Stupidity? Greed?" Christian shrugged.

Sonya tore a copy from the paper she had signed and handed the original to him. "You're very well informed."

"I pick up useless pieces of information from here and there."

She gazed at him levelly. "I'm not sure I believe that."

He tucked the paper into the carefully packed tray that held the collection. "Good," he laughed. "My secret dread is to have people take me seriously."

"Somehow I don't believe that, either."

"Then you're in a bad way. Why don't we stop for a bite to eat before I take you home?"

"You're not taking me home this evening."

"Where else am I taking you?"

"Nowhere. I'm going home alone. On the bus."

"I can't change your mind?"

"No."

He shrugged. "Then, I guess I'll see you tomorrow morning. We'll attack the boxes in Mrs. Richards's garage again. But I'll call her first to make sure we're still welcome."

"Good idea," Sonya said, but she had to muster enthusiasm. Not because the search was so complicated at Mrs. Richards's house but because Christian had seemed almost relieved not to be taking her home. He had offered, but he hadn't insisted or even teased her when she said no. He was treating her exactly as she had longed to be treated, like an ordinary acquaintance.

That was what she wanted, wasn't it?

SONYA DRAGGED HERSELF through the front door and collapsed on the couch. She wasn't so much tired as dispirited. The bus was noisy and dirty, the walk up the hill to their house much too solitary...and she was getting used to having him around.

Sonya shot to her feet. That was a stupid thing to think! She hadn't meant it.

Hildie looked up from where she was curled into the wing chair pulled close to the fireplace. "Something sting you?"

Sonya jumped again. She hadn't been aware that her sister was even in the house. "You frightened me!"

"Sorry."

A hand tugged through her hair.

Hildie closed the book she was studying. "Something wrong?"

"No!" The answer was too quick.

Her sister frowned. "You're all jumpy. Oh! Is it because of Christian Townsend? That was his name, wasn't it?"

Sonya busied herself by taking off her jacket and heading into the kitchen to see what she could find for dinner. "Have you eaten?"

"I've eaten. You didn't answer my question."

"I think I'll have fish sticks. They're pretty quick."

"What's he done now?" Hildie grinned. "Kiss you again?"

"Hildie, please."

"He is something else! Good-looking, smart, and he has a nice laugh."

"You try working with him, then you'll see." That wasn't true anymore. Sonya didn't mind nearly as much as she once had. She, too, was getting caught up in the mysteriousness of the disappearance, not to mention the magnetism of her companion's personality—even though he still overwhelmed her. But she needed something to complain about. She couldn't possibly tell Hildie the truth.

"Did he bring you home? Why didn't you invite him in?"

"Hildie—"

Her sister was grinning broadly when the telephone rang. As usual, she jumped to answer it. But instead of staying on herself, she held it out to Sonya. "For you. I think it's him. Do you want me to tell him you're busy eating a molded fish product?"

Sonya gritted her teeth. Hildie hadn't bothered to cover the mouthpiece. "No. And just you wait. One day, sister mine. One day."

It was a problem that they had only the one telephone, because Hildie made little pretense of returning to her book. She opened it, fixed her gaze on its contents, but never turned a page. Either she had gone completely catatonic or she was preparing to relish every word of Sonya's side of the conversation and fill in the rest for herself.

"Yes?" Sonya said tightly.

"You turned down a wonderful dinner with me for a molded fish product?"

"I happen to like molded fish products."

"Does that mean you don't like me? No, don't answer. I might have my ego crushed."

"Nothing could crush your ego."

"You're angry." When Sonya didn't answer, he said, "You're also edgy. Why?"

"I simply have a headache."

"Then take an aspirin and lie down for a while."

"If you don't mind, I'll take care of my own medical needs."

"I'm just trying to help. Maybe take two aspirins."

"I think I'll take a break . . . from you! I may call in tired tomorrow."

"And leave me with that whole garage to sort through?"

"You deserve it."

The teasing quality that had been in his voice up to that moment changed, becoming much more serious. "I got that call from Sam Peterson. He wants to see us tomorrow morning."

"Why can't he tell you over the phone?"

"He doesn't like phones. Says they're too easily tapped."

"He's paranoid."

"I'm going. Are you?"

Sonya drew a long-suffering breath. "What time?"

The laughter was back in his tone. "I was going to say nine, but since you're in such a weakened condition—"

"I'll be ready at nine."

"If that's what you want."

Sonya made no reply. Instead—damn the thought of rudeness—she hung up the phone without further comment.

Hildie was looking at her from over the top of her book. When she saw that Sonya was in an even worse mood than before, she quickly retreated behind the safety of the pages.

Sonya threw the frozen fish sticks into the toaster oven. They might lodge in her throat—she wasn't the least bit hungry now—but she was determined to eat them.

A short time later, seemingly to spite her, her head began to throb with a dull pain.

SAM PETERSON'S RETREAT from the hectic world clung to the side of a cliff overlooking the Pacific. The cove below could be reached by way of a long series of wooden steps. Huge pillars of rock dotted the incoming surf. On one, a tree clung to life, its limbs so bent by ocean winds that it had become one of Mother Nature's bonsais.

Because the next oncoming front of storms had not yet arrived, Sam showed them to the patio at the rear of his house. Milky rays of sunlight rained down, and the breeze from over the water was unusually mild.

"I'm sure you think I'm overly suspicious, and I probably am, but being safe is a hell of a lot easier than being sorry."

Christian was gazing at the view. "Absolutely gorgeous."

"That's why I bought this place. That and the isolation. I have only two close neighbors and they don't bother anyone. Especially me."

He pulled out a chair and motioned to Sonya. "Here, sit down and I'll get us some drinks. What would you like? I think I can cover almost anything." His worn face screwed into an encouraging smile.

Sonya asked for something cold and soft and Christian opted for the same.

He settled into the seat next to her as they waited for their host to return. "You're feeling better?" he asked, his first personal comment of the day.

She had wondered when it would come. He had been much quieter today than usual. "Much," she agreed.

His gaze settled back on the water and hers followed suit. "Do you feel it?" he asked softly after a moment had passed.

"What?"

"The way things have shifted between us."

Sonya sat very still.

He continued, "You don't seem to resent me as much as you once did and I'm not as suspicious of you."

"Am I supposed to say something to that?" Her heartbeat had quickened, becoming noticeable.

"No. It was just an observation."

Sam returned to the patio, carrying three glasses. He laughed affably as he passed them around. "They're all the same. Take any one."

Sonya's hand was tremulous as she did as he directed. She felt Christian's eyes but would not meet his gaze.

Sam took a long drink. "Ahhh. That really hits the spot. I've been working on my roof. Damned thing had sprung a leak. Had to take advantage of the break in the weather."

Christian glanced at the steep roof. One slip and a person could end up on the rocks waiting far below. "Need any help?" he asked casually.

"Nah. I got it finished just before you came. A couple of shingles on the ridge row were loose and a few others were missing from here and there. Can't say I enjoyed it, though. I don't like heights."

"Heights don't bother me," Christian said. "If we'd known, you could have waited."

"I'll remember your offer."

Sonya stared at the angle of the roof and the distance to the ground and shivered.

After finishing his drink, Sam wiped his mouth with the back of his hand. "I talked with my friend at the lab. There's some good prints on the base of the note. Probably yours, hers . . . mine, for sure. But none on the individual letters. That means that whoever did this was careful. It's not someone acting on a burst of anger. He's methodical and smart. The letters are perfectly cut."

Sonya reached for her purse. "We found where the letters came from. At least, we're pretty sure." She handed the ex-detective the brochure.

He looked at it and nodded. He, too, saw the museum's emblem on the face.

"So what are you trying to tell us?" Christian asked.

"What I said before—watch your backs. This person probably means business."

Sonya felt another shiver pass over her skin. Words of doom? Should they turn the note over to the police officially? But then, if they did, the museum would become involved and the media would find out, exactly what she had been working so hard to avoid.

"I can give you the name of my friend. Normally we don't investigate threats. The caseload is too high. But if I were to send you to him—" He left the rest unsaid.

"We haven't been threatened with any harm," Christian reminded.

"Not yet," Sam added.

Sonya stood up. She couldn't remain still any longer. She walked to the railing that outlined the patio.

The men exchanged a look.

Christian soon followed her. "If you want out," he said quietly, "I'll release you. There's no need for you to put yourself at risk."

"What about you? Are you going to quit?"

"No."

Sonya's hand tightened on the railing. "Then neither am I."

Sam joined them. "If I were you, I'd call my friend."

Christian pulled his gaze away from Sonya. The slight breeze was tugging playfully at her hair, the golden rays of the sun were kissing her skin. She had been looking up at him so earnestly. It was all he could do not to kiss her. He shook his head. "We have our reasons not to."

"Amateurs should never try to do the work of the police. People end up hurt that way...or worse."

"I don't think it will go that far."

"How do you know?" Sam was getting irritated. "You have a crystal ball or something?"

"We'll be careful."

"Famous last words."

Sonya touched the older man's arm. "Thank you for your help, but we have to do this our way. Please try to understand."

The old detective could not resist the sweetness of her plea. His irritation disappeared like ice in a furnace. "At least promise that you'll call me if you do need help. Will you do that?"

"Of course," Sonya assured, smiling at him, and he swallowed convulsively.

"WELL, YOU CAN ADD another scalp to your belt," Christian murmured once they were in the car and headed back to the city.

"What?" Sonya's expression was pensive. She had been deep in thought.

"Poor old Sam. The man didn't know what hit him."

"I wish you'd either explain what you're talking about or shut up."

Christian smiled crookedly. "That's it. Don't save any of the sweetness for me."

"You're babbling."

"I've been doing a lot of that lately, ever since I met you."

Sonya raked a hand through her hair. They had very serious things to think about and there he was being... "Stop being silly. We need to decide what we're going to do."

"About us?"

"About the search!"

"Oh."

He sounded disappointed but he was teasing. She could see it in the grin he was trying to hide. She shifted in her seat. She didn't know who was most dangerous to her, the person who had threatened them or Christian.

She tried to concentrate. "Obviously, we've talked to someone our note writer didn't want us talking to—Mrs. Delia, Mrs. Richards, Sam, the older group of employees at the museum. That's all, isn't it? One of them must be the key."

"Not necessarily. Maybe the person just doesn't want us to get any closer."

"Mrs. Delia was afraid."

"I've given a possible reason for that."

Sonya frowned. "Yes, but—"

Christian slowed the car for a switchback and negotiated it smoothly. "You said you thought Sam was paranoid. I wouldn't go so far as to say that, but he is overly cautious. That comes from too many years on the force. He's seen too much."

"Are you saying you think he's overreacting?"

Christian shrugged.

"Then why did you offer me a way out?" she demanded.

"Because you looked like you wanted it."

Sonya didn't know what to reply. She *had* wanted out, at least at that moment. She had never been threatened before. Her life, except for her parents' divorce, was uneventful, and she liked it that way. The police, fingerprints, threats . . . she was nervous about it all, but if he wasn't going to quit, neither was she. And Ted's directive had little to do with it. She was continuing because she wanted to continue. For no other reason.

"What are we going to do next?" she asked, firming her chin, the question her answer.

Christian flashed an approving smile. "How do you feel about checking out some more Sanskrit?"

LITTLE BY LITTLE the boxes were shifting from the to-be-done stacks to the gone-through stacks. As before, the notes were wonderfully interesting, but they shed little new light on the theft.

Sonya had read aloud Ralph's view of the museum's director at the time. *R. McArthur—pompous ass. Relieved to have a suspect, any suspect. Would claim he saw his own mother steal collection if it would take heat off his precious museum.*

"Ralph was a fine judge of men," Christian offered.

"You met Mr. McArthur?"

"A couple of times, with my uncle."

"Was he pompous?"

"My uncle thought so."

"It's too bad he's dead," she mused.

"Your deep mourning touches me."

"I didn't mean it that way. I meant, if he wasn't dead, we could talk to him."

"Your deep…" he said, starting to repeat his earlier comment, when Flora Richards peeked into the garage.

"Everything was so quiet I wondered if you were still here."

Christian smiled. "We're here, but not for long, if you don't mind us coming back again tomorrow."

"Oh, my, no. You make the place come alive again. Ralph used to spend hours out here puttering around."

"Don't you need to be at the library?" Sonya asked.

"I've taken the week off. I don't have company very often. I like it."

Sonya and Christian exchanged a quick glance.

"But we haven't been much company for you," Sonya said.

"Yes, you have."

Christian straightened, leaving the papers he had been searching through as they were. "Mrs. Richards, go put on your glad rags. Sonya and I are leaving, but we're coming back. We're going to take you to dinner and then dancing."

Mrs. Richards was embarrassed. "Oh, no...no. I wasn't hinting."

"It's our way of thanking you." He flashed a smile and moved over to the woman, pulling her into his arms and circling the clear area of the cement floor in a gliding waltz.

Sonya watched them with amazement. Mrs. Richards was laughing, her astonishment giving way to pleasure. And Christian looked so handsome, his smile both rakish and kind.

Christian twirled the woman to a straightback chair in the far corner of the room. He bowed once when she was seated. "If you would do me the honor of another dance later this evening, madam, you would make me one of the happiest men on earth."

Flora Richards giggled like a schoolgirl. "Well, when you put it like that—"

Christian kissed her hand. "At seven, madam. Sonya and I shall await."

The woman giggled again.

SONYA WAS QUIET as they drove to her home. She had made no protest this time, and when he found a parking place right away again, she no longer thought it so unfair. In her mind all she could see was him twirling the older woman around and around, making her laugh, making her tired eyes sparkle.

"Six-thirty all right with you?" he asked after cutting the engine.

"Yes."

He frowned. "Are you angry that I included you?"

She shook her head. "No."

"Then what is it? What's bothering you?"

She turned to him. Moisture had collected on the tips of her lashes. "That was one of the nicest things I've ever seen anyone do."

He was very still. "I just asked her out to dinner."

"It was the *way* you did it."

"I hadn't thought before that she was so lonely."

"That's what I mean."

"It's not all that big a deal."

"I think it is. You're really a very nice man."

"No."

"You are! Don't ruin it by arguing with me."

Christian frowned. He had always been uncomfortable with the idea of being held to a hero's standard. It was much too difficult to live by. He wanted to be real, very real, especially to Sonya.

When she leaned over to kiss him softly he did not kiss her back. He saw it as a gesture, like a handshake of good will.

Sonya hadn't meant to kiss him, it just happened. She was glad that he hadn't received it as anything other than a token salute. At least, she thought she was.

She let herself out of the car and when she got to the stairs, she turned to wave.

Christian watched her without moving.

SONYA STOOD IN FRONT of her closet door. She had nothing to wear. That was what she got for all those quiet nights at home she had bragged about to Hildie. She checked her watch. She had at least an hour to shop.

CHRISTIAN FOUND HIMSELF staring at the airline ads in the newspaper heralding flights to cities all over the world: London, Paris, Frankfurt, Athens, Rome, Bangkok, Sydney, Tokyo. It would be so easy to book a reservation and walk away. He had friends in most of those cities who would be happy to see him again, and a few past lovers who wouldn't mind, as well.

San Francisco was just one place, one very small city in comparison.

But it was in San Francisco that he stayed.

Chapter Ten

Flora Richards fanned herself breathlessly as she re-took her place at the table. "I haven't had...so much fun in...years!" She was dressed all in pink, from the silk blossoms scattered in her hair to the tips of her pink satin shoes. The dress was more than a few years out of style, but Flora didn't seem to care. She happily told Sonya and Christian that she had last used it at her son's wedding and it hadn't been out of the closet since.

Sonya was wearing a soft peach gown that was deceptively simple in cut. From the first moment she tried it on, she had known that this was the dress she would choose. It complimented her skin, her hair, her eyes and her figure. Hildie had beamed approval when she came out of her bedroom to wait for Christian's arrival.

Christian, of course, was devastating in a tux. His body type was perfect for it, as it was for every other style of clothing Sonya had seen him in. His dark curling hair, his midnight-blue eyes, the dark bronze hue of his skin—

Sonya had felt like Cinderella when he called for her. Flora did, too, but she, at least, had had the honesty to say so.

Christian had laughed at her fancy and made a joke that took attention away from himself.

Sonya was beginning to realize that he did that repeatedly. Whenever too much attention was directed toward him, he neatly took a sidestep, and he did it with such practiced ease that those around him never noticed.

Christian was smiling at Flora's breathlessness. "You could do this every week, if you wanted. I know someone who'd love to bring you, especially when I tell him how good a dancer you are."

"My Ralph loved to dance."

"I'll leave his name with you. He's an old friend of my father's. He lost his wife a year or so ago and is beginning to want to get out again. Could I give him your name, too?"

Flora tittered, then looked at Sonya. "Should I?"

"I don't see why not."

"I don't see why not, either. Donald won't like it, but . . ."

Christian stood up. A new set of music had started to play. He held his hand out to Sonya. Wordlessly, but with a thumping heart, she took it.

Flora sat back in her chair and smiled.

For the start of the slow dance, Christian folded her close. At first Sonya was stiff, her mind reeling with too many sensations: the warmth of his hands, the nearness of his body, his latent strength, the intoxicating scent of his cologne—an overwhelming awareness of *him*! She couldn't follow his lead. Then gradually she began to sense the rhythm of his moves and as he felt her relax, he gathered her even closer.

Sonya's hand was curled against his chest. She could feel his heart beating and the sensation thrilled her. His head was tucked close to hers, intimate in its exclusion of everyone else. His breath was warm against her cheek. She tried not to let herself be seduced by the potency of the moment, though unable to stop, she moved against him.

Christian missed a step. She tried to pull away, but he wouldn't let her.

His hand moved over her back, circling, pulsing.

Sonya trembled.

His lips trailed the sensitive skin of her neck.

Her eyes fluttered shut.

His lips moved to her jawline, to her ear.

Sonya turned her mouth toward his and their lips met, touched, pulled away, met again, parted.

The music stopped.

Christian's hand remained at her back as he escorted her back to the table. In a daze, she sat in her chair.

When she looked at him, he didn't seem at all disturbed, but she knew that it was a lie. His eyes glittered when he met her gaze.

Gradually, she became aware of Flora.

The woman was smiling happily. "I knew you two were more than friends. You just had to be!"

Sonya mumbled an excuse and escaped from the table.

In the bathroom she dampened a paper towel and held it against her face. When she looked in the mirror, she might have been looking at a stranger. Nothing like this had ever happened to her before. Christian was like a drug in her system. The more she was with him, the more she *wanted* to be with him. And the more she wanted to be with him, the more she wanted. Sonya shivered even in the heat of her embarrassment. What was she going to do?

Flora pushed through the door, her kind expression changing to concern as she saw Sonya leaning weakly against the mirror. "Oh, my dear, are you ill? I'll go tell Christian that we have to leave. You've both done much too much for me already." She hurried away without waiting for a reply.

Sonya closed her eyes. She had to get out of this. Did she accept Flora's excuse and plead sudden illness? Christian would know the real reason, but it would put off any further intimacy with him to the future. A future when she would have had time to think.

She dabbed at her forehead before throwing the dampened tissue into a receptacle. Her color had receded until now she was starkly pale. That, along with the stricken hollowness of her eyes, would convince most people that she was feeling unwell. She pulled open the door and stepped outside.

Christian was approaching with the older woman.

"I was just coming in for you," Flora said as she drew near. "Christian is very concerned."

His gaze bored into her, his mouth set in a firm line. There was no trace of his usual teasing either there or in his eyes. His body was taut. "Are you ready to go?" he asked.

Sonya nodded.

THE CHILL NIGHT AIR HELD a great deal of moisture. It hadn't started to rain steadily yet, but it had sprinkled, and the brightly colored lights from the buildings and signs along the street were reflected in the collected moisture on the sidewalk.

Sonya huddled in her coat. Christian was walking between her and Flora, a hand on each of their arms to prevent them from slipping. They turned into the street at the corner near the parking garage.

Halfway across, a horn started to blare. A car, out of control, was careening down the hill, heading straight for them.

For the space of a second Christian froze. Then he swept both Flora and Sonya closer into his arms and lunged forward, using all his strength to propel them out of harm's way. He wasn't sure if his attempt would be successful as he waited for the shock of impact.

The horn was still blaring crazily as the car swept past, swerving away from them at the very last minute. It didn't stop.

Christian's mighty push continued to thrust them toward the opposite sidewalk, as he fought to maintain his balance, and to keep the women on their feet. They clung together in need and fright, each trying to remain upright.

Flora went down first. Christian pulled on her but was unable to stop her fall. He tried his best to break her impact. Then Sonya stumbled, and he twisted, throwing his body beneath her. His left shoulder hit the cement with force.

Passersby hurried over, ready to help, almost before the trio could pick themselves up.

"Are you all right?"

"My God, that car!"

"Did he *try* to hit you?"

Concerned hands reached out to them.

Flora was first on her feet, then hurried over to Sonya and Christian. "Are you hurt? Are you hurt?" she asked, repeating herself in her agitation.

Christian's shoulder was numb. Something hard, a rock, had been lying where he fell. "I'm fine," he lied as his gaze quickly swept over Sonya. Her face was even paler than it had been earlier and her dress was soiled, but she was standing, not looking any more the worse for wear. He switched his gaze to Flora. Her eyes were shining with excitement. Her dress was in even worse shape than Sonya's, but she was chattering to the crowd, obviously enjoying the attention.

"Christian kept us from being killed. He pushed us out of the way, then put me down like a baby," she was telling anyone who would listen. "I didn't even see the car."

He stood up and moved his shoulder stiffly. Feeling was beginning to return, a forerunner of burning pain. He reached for Sonya's hand. Her fingers felt like ice. "Are you all right?" he asked softly.

She nodded, her eyes huge. "You?" she whispered.

He grinned tightly. "I'll live."

Christian found his scarf and accepted the women's purses from the helpful onlookers. "Do you want to call a policeman?" someone asked.

Christian shook his head.

One by one the crowd dispersed.

FLORA ASSURED THEM of her well-being before being left at her house. Possibly a bruise or two, she said, but nothing worse. She had no suspicion that the out-of-control car was anything but a freak occurrence.

Sonya relaxed into the seat of the larger car that Christian had produced for the night. Earlier, she hadn't even bothered to ask if it was his. At the moment she was grateful for the soft leather seats and cushy ride because they comforted her aching muscles. She, too, had been saved from greater harm by Christian's quick action. But there were still places that ached. From the corner of her eye she saw Christian periodically move his left shoulder. She wondered if he was injured more than he had claimed and also wondered about the mystery car that had tried to run them down.

Christian turned to look at her after he cut the engine in front of her house. She felt his gaze run over her.

He fingered a torn seam at the bodice of her dress. "Can it be repaired?"

Sonya hadn't been aware that her dress was ripped and glanced at it. "Probably."

"That was a close call."

"Do you believe it was an accident?"

"Don't you?"

"I don't know."

He sighed. "Don't start reading more into it than what's already there. Something like that must happen frequently in a city like San Francisco. Brakes go out on the hills. People lose control."

"I saw brake lights as the car turned the corner."

Christian was silent. "You think it has something to do with the note?"

Sonya shrugged.

He moved again and this time winced.

"You're hurt!"

"I'm fine."

"Come inside."

Christian looked at her. "If I come in, I might not leave."

"I just want to see your shoulder...take care of it. That's all."

"That might not be all *I* want."

"Come inside," she repeated.

He opened his door. Sonya's hand trembled as she reached for her own.

HILDIE WAS SITTING in the middle of the living room floor, half-done sketches and drawings with swatches of fabric attached scattered all around her.

Christian murmured to Sonya. "You knew, didn't you?"

Hildie jumped up. "What's happened?" she cried, her expression shocked at the change in their appearance.

"We had a little accident," Sonya said before asking Christian for his lightweight coat, then his tux jacket. When he had stripped down to his white pleated shirt, she heard Hildie's quick intake of breath.

"You're bleeding!" her sister cried.

Sonya examined his shoulder. In stark contrast to the white was a wide patch of rich, dark red. She swallowed. "That, too." And motioned for him to continue to strip. "Hildie, get some antiseptic and some warm water in a bowl and a cloth."

"It's really not that bad," he insisted. His shirt had felt wet against his skin, but he hadn't realized that the skin was broken. He had been too involved in controlling the pain to consider it.

He ended up needing Sonya's help to remove the shirt. She carefully pulled it away from the wounded area. The skin was already bruising next to the open gash and blood was trickling down his back.

"Bring some gauze," she called to her sister. "No, bring the box."

The bronze of Christian's tan didn't stop on his chest or back. He was the same sun-kissed color on each section of exposed skin. Short dark hairs swirled on his chest, emphasizing the sculpted muscles.

Sonya felt distinctly giddy and told herself the feeling was caused by the sight of blood. But her eyes kept going back to the beauty of his body. No wonder he looked so good in his clothes.

Hildie ran back into the room, the first-aid kit in her hand. She tossed it to Sonya before hurrying into the kitchen. There was time enough, though, for her to get a look at Christian and blink.

Sonya unwound the gauze. "Tell me if this hurts." She cleaned around the wound. When the warm water arrived, she dipped fresh gauze into it and cleaned the wound itself. Bits of material had to be washed from the raw surface. Christian remained very still as she worked.

Finally, she stepped back. "There, that's all I can do. Maybe a doctor should see this. You might need stitches."

"I doubt it."

"Do you think anything's broken?" Hildie questioned. She had continued to hover close by.

Christian smiled at her. "Nope. It just hurts like hell."

"You suffer nicely," Hildie complimented.

"Thank you." He grinned.

Sonya frowned darkly. "This isn't something to laugh about. We could have been killed!"

Hildie's eyes widened, and Sonya instantly regretted her outburst.

"A car almost hit us," she explained, trying to undo some of the damage. "If Christian hadn't . . ."

"Ifs don't come into it," he interrupted. "The car *didn't* hit us. That's all that counts."

"Do you want a bandage?" Sonya asked, collecting the unused supplies in order to have something to do. She didn't like to think about ifs, either.

He shook his head.

"Maybe you should," Hildie suggested. "If you don't, you'll have to clean it all over again."

"I yield to your better judgment."

"Want me to do it?" Hildie volunteered.

Sonya started to protest then thought better of it and stepped out of the way. She felt Christian's eyes following her.

When Hildie was done, she asked, "Do you need a stiff drink or something? People always ask for that in the movies."

"No, I'll survive on my own now. Thanks."

"As long as you watch out crossing streets."

"I promise to try."

He reached for his shirt and she helped him put it on. He didn't bother to button it.

Sonya watched the entire scene from the corner of her eye. She didn't know which was worse, him partially dressed or him partially undressed.

"See me out, Sonya?" he asked after collecting his discarded clothing.

She wanted to refuse. Too much was happening. Days seemed to have been packed into hours, hours into minutes, and she was experiencing an attraction like none she had ever known before. And it all revolved around one man—a man who sometimes seemed bigger than life.

CHRISTIAN PAUSED ON THE LANDING as she closed the door behind them. With casual unconcern he laid his jacket and coat across the railing. There was a heavier chill in the air and rain had finally started to fall. Still, he seemed uninterested in a quick leave-taking.

Sonya wanted the evening to end. Her mind and emotions were almost past the point of overload. "Yes?" she prompted, on guard, unsure of what was to come. In one way the dance they had shared seemed eons ago, but in another way, it was still there, fresh, in her memory.

"I'm inclined to think you might be right," he said.

She searched her memory. "About what. The car?"

He nodded.

"What changed your mind?"

"You said you saw brake lights."

"Yes."

"I did, too."

She stared at him. "Why didn't you say so before?"

He didn't answer. Instead he said, "Maybe you *should* pull back from this. This changes things from this morning. Then we only had an implied threat. Now it's possible we have more. It's still not proven...maybe it was only a bad driver."

"Then why didn't he stop?" she demanded.

"He was afraid?"

"The coincidence is too high."

"But possible."

She sighed. "Yes."

"Still, I don't want you hurt. Next time, if there is a next time, you might not be able to get out of the way in time."

"Why don't you let me worry about that?"

"Because I feel responsible."

"Well, don't!"

He stepped closer. She wanted to move away but couldn't. She needed to feel his arms around her again, his body pressed close, his lips against hers.

His hand cupped her chin, gently lifting it. "Oh, but I do," he said softly, huskily.

He didn't dally with preliminaries. His kiss was strong and solid and highly charged. Sonya's head started to swim.

His fingers threaded into her hair, his mouth moving over hers, deepening, probing. He rained kisses over her face, her neck, in the hollow between her breasts. That they were covered by the fine material of her dress made little difference. His hands smoothed the curving mounds.

Emboldened by his touch, her hand fluttered to his chest where his shirt was still undone. Her fingers tangled in the short dark hairs, sliding over the muscles, exploring the sensation of touching him.

Each lingering kiss that he gave her, she gave back. Her body was alive to his again. She didn't think about who he was or who she was, or of their different situations in life. There was only this moment, with no beginning and no end.

Ragged of breath, they drew apart. His eyes glittered into hers. "We have to stop," he said. "Either that or we're going to shock your neighbors."

Her laugh was shaky. "You can't shock San Franciscans, haven't you heard that?" She tried to straighten her hair.

"Leave it. I like it mussed. It makes you look—" He didn't complete the sentence. "Where are you going?" he complained softly when she started to pull away. He traced the gentle line of her lips. "Don't. Stay with me a little longer."

"I should go—"

"If Hildie weren't inside, you wouldn't be going in alone. You know that, don't you?"

Sonya hesitated, then nodded.

"I'd like to take you home with me," he said huskily.

A cold fire shot through Sonya's soul. She could go with him, Hildie would understand, but she wasn't ready yet. Her body was, but her mind wasn't, and it was her mind that she would have to live with afterward. She stayed very still, biting her bottom lip to keep from making any sound that he might take as acceptance.

Christian closed his eyes. He knew she wouldn't come, and for the first time since stepping out onto the porch he noticed his shoulder. It must have been aching all along, but he had paid no heed. He moved his arm, trying to loosen the drawing sinews.

"Did we . . . hurt you?" Sonya asked, embarrassed.

His smile was teasing. "No. And even if we had, it was worth it."

He pulled her close again. Sonya tried to remain aloof, but pressing against his length was enough to melt even the most determined soul.

This time when he kissed her, it was with a more restrained passion, caring, sweet and so very special. Dreamy shadows moved in her eyes as they parted.

"Until tomorrow?" he questioned softly, smiling at her.

Sonya swayed slightly, nodding.

Christian didn't want to leave her but knew he must. Another quick kiss and he was gone.

Minutes before, Sonya had stopped noticing the cold. Now each raindrop might have been lovers' tears, shed at the sweetness of parting. Pressing her cheek against one of the carved porch posts, she sighed.

WHEN SONYA REENTERED THE HOUSE, Hildie started to question her, but seeing her sister's state of hazy distraction, she watched with benign amusement as Sonya went directly to her room without uttering a word.

Chapter Eleven

Sonya waited anxiously inside the back door of the museum. From her position she could see most of the area around the steps. Soon, the long dark form she had been waiting for came into view. Without wasting another second, she threw open the door and hurried outside.

When Christian glanced up, he felt his heart jump. Sonya was hurrying toward him, unable to wait for him to cross the short distance that separated them. Even though such an action wasn't like her, he wouldn't complain. After last night, he felt more than a little changed himself.

As she neared, he held out an arm to her. But instead of rushing into his embrace, she grabbed hold and started to pull. "Come on," she said quickly, urgently.

Christian hesitated. "What's wrong? Has someone—"

"Come *on*!" she repeated but was stopped by the arrival of someone else.

When Sonya groaned, Christian realized that the newcomer was the cause of her distress. He turned challenging eyes on the woman.

Millicent Walker blinked and it took her a moment to speak, something Sonya was sure had never happened before.

The reporter quickly recovered. "Miss Douglas... good. I was hoping to speak to you, too."

"We don't have time this morning," Sonya said. "We're expected inside."

The reply was ignored. "Just a few seconds." She turned to Christian. "I've seen you coming and going from here a lot recently. Do you have anything to do with the D'Arcy Gallery or Mitchell Ketchem? A lawyer possibly? One can never be too careful these days with people suing at the drop of a hat... or should I say painting?" She lifted a finely penciled eyebrow at Sonya. "I told you I'd heard something interesting. Why didn't you tell me earlier? I could have given you a prominent place in the article I wrote. As it is, you'll have to wait to be in the second piece. That might be even better, though, because there'll be more readers as the days go on." Her curious gaze traveled back to Christian. "I don't believe I caught your name?"

"That's because I didn't give it."

Sonya tugged on his arm. "We have to go."

He wouldn't budge.

The reporter's ears sharpened. She had detected the concern in Sonya's voice. She turned her full attention on Christian. "Am I right in assuming you're a lawyer?"

"Assume anything you wish," he said softly.

"And that your business here is the Ketchem case?"

Christian was silent.

"I know all about it," Millicent bragged, "so you don't have to try to hide anything. A certain amount of money changed hands. Fifty thousand, it's said, but I happen to know it's more like a hundred."

Again Christian said nothing.

"You're very quiet for a lawyer."

"I have nothing to say."

"Not even a short statement?"

"No."

"Very unlawyerlike. I'm beginning to wonder if possibly I've made a mistake."

"Probably not the first in your career."

The woman gave a sly smile. "That's true. But I'm very careful, otherwise I wouldn't still be doing what I do."

"And exactly what is that?" Christian asked with seeming innocence.

"Ask your girlfriend." After a pause in which neither Christian nor Sonya made a denial, the reporter murmured, "There was a time when I'd have been satisfied to print that, but not anymore. I'm big-time now, and I got there through a hell of a lot of hard work. Gossip doesn't satisfy me, at least, not the boy-meets-girl, boy-sleeps-with-girl kind. It's boring!" She smiled again. "So why don't you tell me what you're up to. It'll make everyone's lives a lot easier."

Christian flashed a dangerous smile. "Life isn't supposed to be easy... or haven't you heard?"

He shifted his hand to Sonya's back and started to accompany her upstairs.

"That works two ways!" the woman called after them, wanting to have the last word.

After they passed safely through the door, Sonya pulled away, her cheeks pink with anger. "I didn't want you to talk with her! She's dangerous, especially when she's been challenged . . . which is exactly what you did!"

"She's on the wrong track, at least as far as we're concerned. If we'd run off, it would have looked even worse, made her more curious."

"She latches on to small things . . . and makes mountains out of them."

"What is she? The best reporter in town? Why aren't any of the others here?"

"She always seems to get here first, then the others follow. Wait until later."

"All the attention might be good for us."

"How?"

"It might keep our friend quiet . . . no more speeding cars."

"Or it might make things worse."

Christian directed her into a small alcove and pulled her against him. "Last night had its good points," he murmured.

Sonya clung to her anger. She had snapped out of her daze somewhere around midnight and was amazed that she had let things get to such a stage between them. She liked her life exactly as it was. She didn't need any disruptions, particularly those caused by a man like him. "Did it? I've forgotten."

Christian smiled. He let her break away and was soon in step beside her. "I could refresh your memory," he offered.

Alarms clanged through Sonya's system. She veered farther away from him, glad that they were nearing the door to her domain. She was even happier when the door opened and Ted Armstrong burst out. Typically, he was breathing fire.

"Have you seen the *Observer* this morning?" he demanded. "It's all over the front page." He waved a mangled newspaper, one that looked as if he had tried to shred it. "San Francisco's own personal tabloid and we've managed to get into it again. We'll sue. This time we're going to sue!"

He didn't wait for them to answer as he stalked off in a continuation of his rage.

ONCE INSIDE HER OFFICE, Sonya dropped into her chair and ran a hand through her hair in agitation.

"Has anyone thought of hiring a detective?" Christian asked as he took up his usual position on the edge of her desk.

"What for?" she questioned.

"To find out who's starting the rumors and who's passing them on. That reporter outside didn't get the story from a little bird. You said she's always the first. She must have a direct line."

"She'd never tell."

"I don't expect she would, but a good detective knows how to get information. It would be worth a try."

"Ted would never hear of it. He'd be afraid that word would get out and make the museum look even worse. As if it could."

"What about a private party?"

"I don't—" She stopped and looked at him with widening eyes. "You don't mean— But why? Why should you care?"

"For truth... justice... and the American way? Is that good enough?"

"You have delusions of grandeur."

His smile was crooked. "Not really."

"Then why not hire someone to find out who stole your uncle's collection? I'm sure a private investigator could do a much better job of it than us."

"And take the chance of having word get out on that, too? You're forgetting—the Townsend collection is real. The museum can weather a lie. It can't live down the truth."

"And you *want* to do it yourself."

"Exactly."

Sonya looked away. Maybe she could get a transfer to some small museum in a nice little town where the most exciting thing that happened was the twice-yearly library used-book sale.

"Let me worry about it," he said. "I'll do what I think is right. No one else need know."

"But why? Why should you...?"

He leaned over to kiss her lips quiet. When he drew back, he teased, "You want to try that again?"

Sonya decided it was a good thing she was already sitting down.

WHEN THEY LEFT THE MUSEUM a short time later, they had to wend their way through a gathering mass of reporters. Television personnel from the local stations were busy videotaping that evening's reports on the museum's latest difficulties, and a representative from the print media recognized Sonya and tried to speak with her, but Christian intervened and the reporter changed his mind.

Sonya settled into the car with a grateful sigh then chanced a quick glance at Christian. He didn't look the least ruffled, but she was beginning to recognize that that was a facade he assumed. As a protection? No, he wasn't insecure. But he did hesitate to reveal himself to prying eyes—most times even to her eyes.

But then, why shouldn't he? What was she to him? Merely an acquaintance? Someone who could provide help in attaining a goal while at the same time attaining a goal of her own?

It was more than that, though. Their relationship wasn't that simple and it was this compilation of complications that was beginning to worry her.

FLORA WAS HAPPY to see them again. She had discovered that her ankle was a bit on the tender side this morning when getting out of bed, but that was the worst of her complaints. And them? she asked.

Sonya murmured that she was fine and felt guilty because she hadn't even asked about Christian's shoulder. There hadn't been much of an opportunity, but she should have asked. She listened with undue attention as he answered the older woman's inquiry.

"A little stiff," he said. "Not bad, though."

"We owe you so much. I haven't told Donald, but I'm not sure that I'm going to. He might try to keep me from going dancing again. And I want to. I enjoyed myself tremendously last night. Up until..." Her words trailed away.

"We all did. Right, Sonya?"

Sonya smiled tightly.

Flora looked from one to the other. She sensed that everything was not as it should be. "I'll leave you to it," she said quietly. "You'll never get work done with me taking up so much of your time. I'll bring coffee later."

"Great," Christian agreed.

SONYA COULDN'T WORK as happily today as she had in the past. The trouble the museum was experiencing was on her mind as well as her own troubles. She needed a vacation, she needed Christian to leave her alone—neither of which was going to happen. And the worst thing was she didn't want him to.

Several times she directed a furtive glance his way, and each time he was intent upon what he was doing, frowning slightly as he tried to decipher a particularly difficult form of Ralph Rogers's shorthand.

He looked so devastatingly handsome, even as he concentrated. She remembered what it was like to touch him, to be touched by him. A flow of warmth shuddered over her.

Could it be that he was playing a game with her?

SONYA STRETCHED after what had to be an hour and rubbed her eyes. It was then she noticed that Christian was very still, reading through the lines of a small notebook. He looked up when he felt her gaze. A slow smile touched his lips. "I've found something."

Sonya hurried over, falling to her knees at his side. "What is it?"

He pointed to the page. "Right there."

Sonya read aloud the abbreviated words. *"Chan. The Shop of the Monkey. Knows Townsend connection from past."* Her gaze lifted. "Who's Chan? Did your uncle know someone by that name? Or is it an abbreviation, too? For Chandler? Or Channing?"

Christian shrugged. "I have no idea." He searched the area around them. "I wonder if Flora has a telephone book."

"I'll see."

Sonya was on her feet and hurrying to the door into the house when Christian stopped her. "Over there. On the shelf next to the washing machine. I thought I remembered seeing one before."

Sonya changed direction. "It's old," she called after pulling it down and reading the date. "About five years."

"That doesn't matter. What we're looking for is even older."

Sonya settled next to him with the thick book. "We should look up The Shop of the Monkey. There'll be too many Chans." She flipped through the yellowed pages, found the *S*'s, then narrowed her search further. Her finger stopped on the exact name. "It's here."

Rising, Christian took the book. "Let's borrow Flora's phone."

Sonya was struggling to her feet again when he reached down to help her. His fingers, curling around hers, were warm and strong and he didn't immediately let go when she had gained her footing.

Sonya's heartbeat quickened. If this *was* a game, she very badly wanted to play. But how devastated would she be when it was over?

He led the way into the house, having tapped on the door and received Flora's permission to enter. She was thrilled to learn that they might have found the information they had been searching for.

Christian dialed the listed number. A moment later he was speaking halting Chinese. Sonya and Flora exchanged glances.

He laughed as he switched back to English. "Yes. Much better, thank you. It's been a long time." He paused, listening, then said, "I'm calling for Mr. Chan. Is he available?" He listened again. "Last year?" Another pause. "Does he have a telephone? No? Well, how could I contact him then?" Finally, he slipped again into Chinese, giving what had to be an expression of gratitude or departure before hanging up.

"What did he say?" Sonya asked, unable to wait.

"She," he corrected. "There is a Mr. Chan. Last year he became too frail to work in the shop, so now he stays in the family home. She gave me directions. It's in Chinatown, in a set of rooms above the shop. She's his granddaughter."

"What's stopping us, then? Let's go."

"He won't see us until evening."

Sonya sighed.

"Anyway," Christian smiled, "we have to clear up our mess in the garage. Flora, I don't know how we can ever thank you."

"Oh, anytime... anytime. I've enjoyed it."

IT TOOK ANOTHER HOUR to put the boxes back into the positions they were in before they had started to go through them, being careful to separate the remaining few they had yet to search, in case this wasn't the lead they thought it was. And parting from Flora took even longer. She insisted upon serving them a light lunch. It was she who asked the question Sonya had determined not to.

"Chinese is such a difficult language, Christian. Wherever did you learn it?"

"My family lived in Hong Kong for a few years when I was growing up. It was hard not to pick it up."

"Hong Kong!" Flora exclaimed. "I've always wanted to go there."

"Then why don't you?" he asked, smiling.

"Why? Well, I don't know. I've just—I'm getting much too old to go gallivanting across the globe, don't you think?"

"Isn't the saying... you're only as old as you feel? If you're hesitant to go alone, you could always travel with a tour group. The company makes all the arrangements and looks out for you, seeing that everything moves smoothly. They want to be sure you're having fun."

"I don't know—"

"The world is a beautiful place, Flora."

"You make me feel so young again. Like I could do anything!"

"That's you, not me. Maybe you should listen to what you really want."

Flora's lined face began to beam. "Maybe I will!"

ONCE IN THE CAR, Sonya thought about what Christian had said—*listen to what you really want*. But in life, weren't there usually too many obstacles?

Maybe not for him... She glanced at him. He looked content, confident. Did insurmountable obstacles ever get in his way? Or, as wealthy as he was, could he shift them with the force of numerous dollar bills? No problem... no sweat... just a wish? Not to mention the way he looked and the force of his personality. Altogether, a formidable combination.

"Why don't you come to my place for dinner tonight?" he asked, turning to glance at her.

Sonya immediately shook her head. "No."

"My sister will be there. It won't be anything elaborate. After we get back from talking to Mr. Chan."

Sonya still didn't agree.

"Are you afraid again?" he chided softly.

He got the desired result. "I'm not afraid," she denied.

"Then?"

"What about your sister? She won't mind?"

"It was her idea."

Sonya looked away. Hearing that made her nervous. He had talked about her? What had he said? "I don't know," she prevaricated.

His hand left the steering wheel to smooth some stray hairs at the side of her cheek. "Say yes," he urged.

Sonya swallowed. She was like a moth fighting against the flame of her own desire. "All right," she heard herself agree.

His fingers traveled to the sensitive skin of her neck, causing her to shiver. From presentiment of what was to come?

SONYA TRIED TO CONCENTRATE on the papers spread out on top her desk. Christian had told her he had some personal business to take care of and wouldn't be back at the museum until shortly before the time they were to leave to talk to Mr. Chan. Since she had the free time, Sonya had decided to try to make use of it again by clearing the leftover paperwork. But she was accomplishing little. Too much was happening, both within and without the museum, for anyone to get much work done.

Barbara had already come in and out of her office several times, worrying about the security of all their jobs, and another one of her assistants had to leave with a migraine brought on by the pressure under which he was trying to work.

Sonya pushed the papers away. It was impossible.

When she looked up, it was to see David standing hesitantly in her doorway. A smile of relief tilted her lips as she got up to pull him farther into the room. "Come in...come out of the storm...and talk to me! It's been so long." She closed the door behind him, giving them a measure of privacy.

David still looked uncomfortable. "I wasn't sure if I'd be welcome."

"You're always welcome, David. You know that."

He took a seat but still did not completely relax. "You've been so busy—"

"I'm not now."

"Has he given up?"

There was no need to ask to whom he was referring. "No."

David looked down at his hands. "I wish he would."

"Why?"

"I don't think I should answer that."

Sonya changed the subject. If David was trying to keep the peace between them, she would too. "Have you read Millicent Walker's article in the paper? Is it as bad as everyone says?"

He looked up, shaking his head. "She rips us apart."

"Ted claims we're going to sue."

"I doubt if he'll have a leg to stand on. She makes her point very carefully."

"Christian thinks someone is feeding her information from inside the museum."

David snorted. "He would!"

"Why don't you like him, David?" Sonya hadn't meant to ask the question so directly, but since she had, she let it stand.

The curator frowned. "I don't like what's been happening since he arrived."

"But he hasn't *done* anything. None of this is his fault."

"Now *you're* defending him."

"If you were in his place, wouldn't you want to find out what had happened to a relative's collection all those years ago? I can't really say I blame him. I'm sure I'd feel the same way."

"He should leave well enough alone."

"You sound exactly like some of the people we've talked to! Don't let any light in . . . who knows what it might reveal. But, David, light *has* to be let in. Otherwise . . ."

David jumped from his seat to grasp her shoulders. "I don't like it that he's using *you*! People like him are all the same. They think that because they're privileged they can run roughshod over everyone else. They take what they want and no one is supposed to object. Well, I *do* object. I object strenuously!"

Without him being aware of it, his fingers were tightening into her flesh, bruising her. She tried to move away, but he held her firmly.

"David," she complained.

He didn't hear. "I'm not going to let him hurt you, Sonya. I've seen the way he looks at you. The way he . . ."

Sonya pried at his fingers. "David! That hurts!"

He instantly let go, shocked that he had hurt her. "I'm sorry . . . I'm sorry. I didn't mean—" He flushed and avoided her gaze, then hurried out the door to escape down the hall.

Sonya's hands cupped her shoulders while her eyes were riveted on the doorway. She couldn't believe that David had behaved so badly. What had happened to the gentle, humorous man whom she thought she had known? What had caused him to— It was almost as if he were jealous!

Sonya gave a low moan. She liked David. She had from the first day they had worked together. But love him? At question, though, weren't her feelings but his. Was jealousy the root cause of his dislike for Christian?

She slumped back into her chair. Why did so many difficult-to-solve problems have to show up now, when she could least afford the energy to solve them?

Chapter Twelve

Christian could sense Sonya's distraction. It was funny, but almost unwittingly he had become aware of every little thing about her. The way she moved her hands when emphasizing a point, the flash of anger in her eyes when challenged, the tiny dimple that came and went in her right cheek when she smiled, the manner in which she held her mouth when wrestling with a problem . . . as she was doing now.

"Would you like to talk about it?" he asked.

"What?" She had been startled from her thoughts.

"Whatever's bothering you . . . do you want to talk about it?"

"Nothing's bothering me."

He shrugged.

Silence again stretched between them in the car. After a moment, Sonya said, "It's nothing you can do anything about, so there's no reason for you to know."

"Does it have to do with the museum?"

"One part, yes."

"There's more than one part?"

She gave him a disgruntled look. "Isn't there always? Or wouldn't you know about that? Do problems always neatly line themselves up for you, one after the other...if they even dare to present themselves at all?"

He spared her an irritated look. "What weird kind of creature do you think I am? I have two arms, two legs, a brain, blood in my veins...but none of that seems to count."

"I didn't mean..."

"If you don't want to talk about your problems, you don't have to."

He directed the car into a parking place.

"Christian—"

"Save it. If you change your mind later, we'll talk. If not, no great loss."

Sonya blinked back a sudden sting of tears. She had no idea why she should feel so hurt by his rejection, especially since she had just rejected him. But she hadn't meant to be so caustic. It had just slipped out. *He* seemed to have meant what he said.

As he got out of the car, she quickly wiped her eyes. She didn't want any trace of moisture to reveal her vulnerability. If he could hold himself aloof, so could she.

He was at her door before she was ready. She stuffed the tissue back in her purse and got out. To compensate, she held her head high.

Christian took her arm but made no further attempt to talk with her.

CHINATOWN WAS ALIVE WITH PEOPLE, tourist and native alike. Even as dusk approached, bins and tables were set out on sidewalks and people were hawking their wares. Children played among the crowds, their happy voices mingling with the songlike speech of their elders, many of whom switched from Chinese to perfectly unaccented English with ease. Narrow alleyways were crowded with boxes and people preparing for the upcoming New Year celebration and parade. Costumes were being inspected, drums tried out, roles rehearsed.

Christian led the way into a tiny shop where ivory carvings, porcelain, brass and jade objects were on display.

The young woman behind the counter was delicately beautiful: fine bones, clear skin, dark almond eyes, long dark hair. Her overblouse was made of blue silk, her pants straight and black. Her makeup was perfectly applied.

Christian went directly to her. "We've come to see Mr. Chan. Was it you I talked to earlier?"

A shy smile touched her lips.

Christian smiled warmly in return, and Sonya was rocked by a rush of jealousy so strong that she had no trouble recognizing it for what it was. The Chinese woman was so young and beautiful. She was more Christian's type: mysterious, exotic. Sonya's own inadequacies seemed magnified.

The young woman said something in Chinese and motioned for them to follow.

She led the way through the back of the shop to a quiet alleyway where an exterior flight of stairs rose to a third level. Sonya wanted to hold back, to wait, to examine the chaos of her feelings, but Christian gave her fingers a bracing squeeze before starting to climb the stairs.

"My grandfather has been ill," the young woman explained. "He enjoys visitors, but please, do not stay long."

She opened the door to a room off the second floor landing, then smiled shyly again before going back to the shop.

The room they entered was large and almost completely dark. Furnishings were only vague images except for an ungainly hospital bed that was lighted by a small reading lamp attached to the wall above. In it, a fragile-looking man was napping.

Christian hesitated, Sonya close to his side.

The old man opened his eyes. He looked at them for a moment before motioning for them to come closer. "My granddaughter tells me you wish to speak with me." His voice was dry with age and weakness. "Tell me, have we met?"

Christian settled a chair for Sonya before choosing one for himself. "No, sir. We never have. But someone led us to you. A man named Ralph Richards. He was a reporter for..."

"I remember him," the man interrupted. "You are a friend of his?"

"No, we never met. Unfortunately, he died some years ago. We found your name in one of his notebooks."

The man waited.

Christian continued, "We were hoping that you might be able to help us."

"In what way?"

"A number of years ago, an exhibit was stolen from the Wortham Museum. It belonged to a man named Townsend. In his notes, Ralph Richards wrote that you know of a connection to the past."

The old man didn't move.

"We wish to know what that connection is," Christian said.

Still the old man didn't move. Sonya began to wonder if something had happened to him, until he blinked, saying, "That was many years ago."

"Yes."

"Why do you wish to disturb the past? To make a profit? Why?"

Christian leaned forward. "Professor Townsend was my uncle."

The man sighed. "I understand now." He paused, breathing deeply. "I am an old man, about to face the end of my life. Your uncle?"

"He died recently."

The old man nodded. "Once, long ago, I traveled to meet a friend. He was assisting your uncle at a small village in Italy. It was both my first trip away from San Francisco and my last. I have never forgotten it.

"I am a humble man. I do not ask and I do not expect to receive. My grandfather came here from China. He worked to make a home so that he could bring my grandmother here. When finally she came, he was happy. He had made a good life.

"I, too, have made a good life. I have four sons, six grandsons and nine great-grandsons."

"You met my uncle?" Christian prompted.

"He was a kind man."

"Who was your friend? In what way did he work with my uncle?"

"He helped to move the dirt around. He helped to find hidden objects."

"Where in Italy was this? Do you remember?"

"Not far from Rome. The bus ride was short."

"How is this a connection?" Sonya asked, no longer able to keep herself out of the conversation. She felt the old man's eyes settle on her. He was so thin and wrinkled, he might have been a thousand years old.

"My friend worked at the museum."

"What was his name?" Christian asked.

"Anson James."

Sonya remembered the name, having seen it on the list of past workers who were no longer in the museum's employ.

"How did you become involved?"

"My friend did not want anyone to know that he had worked with your uncle. He pretended to be sick when your uncle visited after the theft. But after your uncle left, Ralph Richards was still here. He asked many questions. My friend pretended ignorance. I could not pretend when Mr. Richards came to question me. I told him nothing, but he remained curious."

"Have you talked with this friend of yours lately?"

"No, the years—"

As he answered, the old man's voice grew noticeably weaker, his strength waning.

Christian stood up. He touched the old man's parchmentlike hand. "Thank you, Mr. Chan. You've been a great help." Then, in Chinese, another phrase.

The old man smiled before becoming still again.

WHEN THEY LEFT THE APARTMENT, they found that the alleyway was no longer deserted. Someone in a one-person lion costume was now practicing his art in the seclusion. Up and down the great, colorful head moved, shaking ferociously from side to side. A bright yellow skirting covered most of the man's body, except for his lower legs, and dragged on the ground behind him.

Sonya turned to Christian as they neared the bottom of the stairs. "What exactly do you think Ralph suspected? That Anson James had something to do with the disappearance? Or Mr. Chan? Or both?"

Christian shrugged as they gained the cobblestones below.

"Do you think we should keep looking in his papers?" she asked. "There are so few left."

Christian started to make a reply when he noticed that the lion was dancing much closer. The head continued to bob up and down and shake. The man inside seemed not to notice that they were there. Christian reached for Sonya's arm, ready to pull her back if necessary. The wall at their side was solid. There was no doorway.

Sonya started to repeat her question when suddenly she stopped. The lion had hit her! Not hard, but enough to sting.

Christian heard her startled intake of breath. He called, "Hold on, there!" But the lion didn't yield. It kept coming, pushing them hard against the wall.

Christian's hold tightened on Sonya's arm. He would not let them be separated.

The lion lunged, then a foot shot out, hitting Christian in the knee. He oofed in pain, doubling over. The lion shook itself and lunged at Sonya.

Christian dived forward, diverting the animal from its course. Material tore, his hands losing their grip.

The lion skipped back. Then it became still and from inside the depths of the great head a voice, low and urgent, said, "I warned you to leave well enough alone. You wouldn't listen. Next time I won't miss. You can expect the worst." Then the figure turned and ran from the alley.

Christian tried to run after it, but his knee was hurting so badly that he couldn't. He made it to the street in time to see the lion disappear into a crowd at the far end of the block.

Sonya was at his back, her breathing short from fright. "My God!" She panted. "I can't believe—"

Christian leaned back against a storefront window and murmured, "I seem to keep having trouble with lions."

Sonya shot him a disbelieving look. He could joke? At a time like this?

He lifted her hand and examined it. "At least the skin's not broken."

"What about you?"

He flexed his leg. His knee still ached. "I'll live."

Sonya glanced in the direction the lion had taken. "At least we have one question answered."

"What's that?"

"He isn't old."

Christian laughed shortly. "Either that or he's in the Senior Olympics."

"Did you recognize the voice?"

"I was just going to ask you that."

She shook her head.

Christian was still limping as they started to move down the sidewalk. Seeing his difficulty, Sonya offered unspoken aid, and they looked like the other couples strolling along with their arms wrapped tightly around each other.

"I think it's someone trying to protect someone else," Sonya said as they stopped at the car.

Christian dug for his keys and unlocked the passenger door. "Can you drive a stick shift?"

Sonya blinked. "Yes."

He tossed the keys to her. "It'll be safer."

Sonya watched as he folded himself into the passenger seat, then went to the driver's side and slid into the seat. The car had an entirely different perspective from this side. It felt powerful even before the engine was switched on. "It's been years, and I've never driven a Porsche."

"We'll chance it."

Power vibrated through her fingertips as the engine caught. She swallowed and carefully pressed in the clutch. The gears meshed smoothly as she shifted into first. But she gave the engine too much gas and they drew attention as they lurched away from their parking slot.

When Christian chuckled softly, Sonya, embarrassed, gave him a warning look. "Just remember that this wasn't my idea."

"I'll remember."

"Which way do I turn?"

"Left. Then right at the next street. Then keep going awhile. I'll tell you what to do after that."

Sonya had to admit that she enjoyed driving the car. It was like sitting on the back of a barely tamed animal. As her coordination got smoother, more practiced, she negotiated each successive turn with more ease.

Christian absently rubbed his knee, a half smile of appreciation on his lips. She tried to cling to the image of stiff control and propriety, but underneath beat the heart of a woman willing to take chances. Another woman might have begged off continuing the search, both after the near miss with the car and now this much stronger threat. But Sonya had not.

"Why do you think it's someone trying to protect someone else?" he asked belatedly, following up on her earlier statement.

She had become comfortable enough with her driving ability to glance at him. "It seems logical, and I can't think of any other reason."

"What about money?"

She frowned. "I don't know what you mean."

"This afternoon, after I left you at the museum, I located someone who will be very discreet. I advanced him some money and will pay him more if he comes up with any useful information."

"An investigator."

"Correct. Why can't whoever's responsible for the theft have done the same thing?"

"You think the person threatening us has been hired?"

"It's possible."

She was silent. "How seriously should we take this latest . . . threat?"

"Pretty serious. Turn left here."

"But you're not going to stop."

"*I'm* not, no. Turn right."

She tilted her head. "Exactly what do you mean by that?"

"Go halfway up the block. The drive with carved lions on the pillars in front . . . yes I know. Lions again."

She would not be diverted. "I'm still interested in what you said."

"I'm going to continue alone."

"No."

She swung into the drive. A huge house was set a short distance from the street on a generous lot that boasted both a yard and a detached garage—something very valued in a city as crowded as San Francisco. The view from the hill overlooked the Pacific as it narrowed into the bay, a perfect vista of one of the prettiest sites in the area.

Sonya refused to be impressed. After cutting the engine and applying the emergency brake, she turned to him and said, "If it's too dangerous for me, then it's too dangerous for you. Do as Sam Peterson said, involve the police."

"I'd rather not."

"Then I'd rather not stop, either."

"Why not?"

Sonya saved herself from answering right away by getting out of the car.

Once outside he caught up with her. "Why not?" he repeated.

"I'd just rather not, okay? Leave it at that."

He tugged on her arm, stopping her. Night had fallen as they drove the short distance from Chinatown and the air was heavy with moisture again. A storm front was close off shore, promising the blessing of rain to a region that had to store its winter bounty for the long arid months of summer and fall.

"Is it because you've come to feel something for me?" he probed.

Sonya was glad for the darkness and tried to pull away.

"Sonya," he said softly.

Response shook through her. It was stronger this time than it had ever been. She jerked her arm away and hurried to the porch. When he came up behind her, he stood close, touching her, trying to make her turn to him.

She resisted. "No!"

His hand fell away.

Sonya slowly turned, looking at him through the diffused light coming from the windows. Then a brighter light was switched on, momentarily revealing everything.

The front door was pulled open by a woman of breathtaking beauty. Dark hair, dark eyes, she was wearing a dress of white silk. "I thought I heard a car," she said.

Letitia's gaze swept over her brother and the woman at his side. If she noticed the strain between them, she didn't remark on it. She stepped out of the way so that they could enter.

The entryway was massive, its ceiling higher than two ordinary floors. A great chandelier emitted sparkling light.

Sonya moved stiffly, trying to avoid Christian's gaze. In the moment before the door opened, there had been something naked in his look, something vulnerable.

"We're not late, are we?" he asked, completely composed again.

"Since you told me seven-thirty and it's not that time yet, no. Aren't you going to introduce us?"

"If you'd give me half a chance, yes. Sonya, my sister Letitia."

As a warm hand reached out to envelop hers, Sonya felt dark eyes travel over her. A murmured exchange of words followed and Letitia then led the way into another room.

"Christian tells me that you work at the museum. I find that very interesting. Is it interesting for you?"

Sonya was awed by the size of this room, as well, and by the decor. It looked like something out of a magazine, all rich woods and shining crystal, yet it was warm, welcoming. "Yes, yes it is."

"And you're working with him concerning the disappearance of our uncle's collection."

Sonya nodded. "Yes."

Letitia indicated the floral-patterned couch and chairs. Each took a seat . . . Sonya highly uncomfortably.

"My brother tells me very little," Letitia complained. "Possibly I can learn more from you."

In spite of her determination not to, Sonya glanced at Christian. He was right at home in this setting, with his perfectly pressed pants and pristine white shirt that wouldn't dare wrinkle or get soiled. He met her look levelly and her heart gave a small flip. She dragged her eyes away.

"Yes," she said again and cleared her throat to expound when she realized that that one word had been the backbone of her conversation since entering the house. She scrambled for something else to say. "Your—your home is very beautiful."

Letitia smiled slightly. "It's not my home. Not really. I stay mostly in London in a flat overlooking the Thames." She looked around. "This is beautiful, though." Her gaze settled on her brother. "Why don't you get us all a drink? Oh! I think we're out of vermouth. There's a bottle in the pantry. I saw it earlier but forgot to bring it."

Christian lifted a brow in whimsy. "You've been nosing around in the pantry?"

"I was checking to see if we had a certain spice for our dessert tonight. It's something special. We didn't, so Carmel had to go out. Don't make fun or I won't let you have any."

Christian gave a half smile before turning to Sonya. "Do you have a preference?"

She shook her head.

"You're usual?" he asked his sister.

She nodded and impatiently swung her crossed leg, almost, but not quite, tapping her toe against the floor.

Once they were alone, Letitia stopped swinging her foot and leaned forward conspiratorially. "I've been so anxious to meet you," she said, smiling. "I asked Chris to bring you earlier, but this was the first time he agreed. Actually, it surprised me when he called. I thought he was going to keep you a secret all to himself."

Sonya didn't know what to say.

Letitia continued. "I wanted to meet the woman who's having such an odd effect on my brother."

"Surely you don't mean me."

"Who else would I mean?" Letitia reached for a cigarette, lighted it, then asked belatedly, "Do you mind?" But she didn't wait for an answer. "He's definitely not his usual self. To others he might be, but not to me. I know him too well. He's more . . . quiet, introspective."

Sonya felt quite warm. The air had grown suddenly heavy. "Possibly it's the situation," she suggested.

"I thought that at first, but now I don't. No. It's you. I feel it whenever he says your name. I think he's falling in love with you." Letitia continued, "It won't last, of course. I keep trying to tell him we have a family curse, but he won't listen to me."

Christian came back into the room, carrying a bottle. He immediately saw Sonya's agitation and shot his sister a questioning look.

Letitia smiled brightly. "I was just asking Sonya if she knew that you had an exhibit in her museum...part of the treasure from those two Spanish ships you and your friends raised in the Gulf. It was divided between several museums, wasn't it?"

Sonya's gaze flew to Christian. One surprise always seemed to lead to another with him. "Is that true?" she whispered.

"If you're trying to help, Letitia, you're certainly going about it in the wrong way. If you're not...."

"Christian!" she pouted.

"I—I have to go," Sonya said. "I don't feel very well. Thank you for the invitation to dinner, but—" She couldn't finish the excuse. Anyway, Letitia didn't want one. She had known exactly what she was saying and doing. Sonya could see it in her eyes.

"What else did you say to her?" Christian demanded.

"Nothing," his sister replied.

Sonya hurried to the door.

On his way after her, Christian paused to say, "Now I understand why Misha said he wanted to kill you at times."

"But I didn't mean for..."

Christian didn't wait to listen. Instead, he ran after Sonya, catching up with her a short distance down the sidewalk.

"I'll drive you home," he said.

Sonya's back was stiff. "I can get a cab."

"Not with our nut case on the loose."

"No, I . . ."

"Get in the car."

He pushed her inside and went round to the driver's side.

As they pulled away, the silence between them grew. Finally, he asked, "What did she say to you? It wasn't just about the exhibit, was it?"

"Just take me home, please."

Christian's fingers tightened on the steering wheel. "She's my sister and I love her dearly, but sometimes it's best if we're on opposite sides of the world. I'm sorry she upset you."

"She didn't."

"Don't lie to me!"

"I was already upset, okay?"

He forced himself to calm down. In a steady voice he reminded, "I did ask if you wanted to talk about it."

"And I said I'd rather not!"

Christian knew there was no use pushing the situation any further. Only more harm would come of it.

THIS TIME THERE WAS no empty parking place in front of Sonya's house. Christian had to circle the block several times before finding one a distance down the hill.

Once they were parked, Sonya remained in her seat. She wanted to get out of the car but couldn't. She sensed that if she did, something essential to her life would be lost.

Letitia had said that he was falling in love with her. Impossible. She had also said that it wouldn't last. How did *she* know?

But *love*?

Sonya pressed a hand to her stomach. Her life was getting so complicated. Less than two weeks ago she had been happy in her work, happy in herself. Then he had come.

"Sonya?" He called her name with such softness that she caught her breath.

"Sonya, look at me."

She shook her head. "I can't deal with anything more right now, Christian. Please. Not now. Maybe tomorrow."

He badly wanted to touch her. Hold her. Kiss her. But he held himself in check.

Sonya's emotions were such a mass of contradictions. If he touched her, she didn't know what she would do. Part of her wanted him to, badly—just to see; another part of her was afraid.

Unconsciously solving the predicament, he opened his door and stepped outside. Sonya watched as he came around to open her door. For several long moments he stood there, looking at her. Then, unsmiling, he offered her his hand.

Was it symbolic that she eventually took it?

There had been no commitment, no words, but they had exchanged something.

Chapter Thirteen

Letitia fingered the small green bottle that sat on their father's desk behind which Christian sat. Her expression remained pouty.

"I don't see why you're so angry. I merely told her the truth. I thought she should be warned. It's not easy to love someone, especially one of us."

Christian looked up from the letter he was reading. "Gillian is getting married. Another naturalist."

Letitia made a face. "He probably looks like a camel. That's all she's interested in right now."

"Well, if he makes her happy—"

Letitia set the bottle down with a thump.

"Hey!" Christian cautioned. "Watch out!"

"Oh, I don't care about your old things. They're stupid. They always have been. People shouldn't live in the past. Only the present."

"Why don't you go back to London? See if you can find Misha."

"I don't *want* to find Misha."

"He probably won't make the first move."

"I'd rather die."

He gazed at her consideringly. "You're not happy here." When she paced to the bookcase, he spoke to her back. "Go to London. Talk to him."

She whirled around. "Are you trying to get rid of me? All because of what I said to your little friend?"

"It's not that and you know it. Anyway, I still don't know exactly what you said to her."

"I told her about the curse."

"Oh, Letitia."

She bit her bottom lip. "I was lonely."

"That's what I'm trying to tell you! You said when you first came here that you still loved him. If you do, do something about it."

"It's not as easy as that! You'd know, if only you..." She stopped, met his gaze and looked away. "I'm sorry," she murmured. "I didn't mean to mess everything up."

"I don't think you have."

She moved back to the desk and tipped his dark head back until he could do nothing but look at her. "So you *do* love her?"

He hesitated. "I'm not completely sure."

"I am. I've watched you with her."

"I'm glad *you're* sure," he teased.

She bent to kiss his forehead. "I'm going to give you the same advice as you gave me. If you love her, *do* something about it."

SONYA STARED AT THE RAIN falling quietly on the street. The worst of the storm was over. The wind had blustered; a muted clap of thunder had sounded in the distance. Now all that was left were the gentle rain-drops, the aftermath of emotion.

An unheeded tear rolled down her cheek. The weather fitted her mood perfectly.

A tap sounded on her door and Hildie peeped inside. "You're awake, too?" she ventured.

Sonya nodded, wiping at her cheek.

As she had when she was younger, her sister snuggled next to her on the window seat, a quilt wrapped about her slender form. For a time they were both quiet, watching the rain. Then Hildie sighed. "It's hard to know what to do sometimes, isn't it?"

"Very," Sonya agreed.

"Especially when it concerns the rest of your life."

Sonya nodded.

"All the responsibility," Hildie said, and was quiet again. Then, "I'm going to finish this term at school . . . then, I don't know. I know you think I'm talented, but I see what the other people are doing and mine looks so strange. It's out there all by itself, and my teachers kind of look at me like they're wondering what planet I came from."

"Maybe they're impressed," Sonya suggested.

"I think they're too nice to tell me it stinks."

"Teachers don't usually have that problem."

"My stuff's so weird it confuses them."

"I don't think it's weird."

"You're my sister."

Sonya put an arm around Hildie's shoulders and hugged her. She, too, remained silent until she sighed.

Hildie studied her in the weak light. "You look so sad," she whispered. "You want to talk about it?"

Sonya shrugged.

"Does it have anything to do with Christian?"

Sonya's body tightened, signaling Hildie that she was right.

"Does it— Are you . . . in love with him?"

It took Sonya a moment to answer. "Probably."

"You don't know for sure?"

"I am...I do. But what good is it going to do me?"

"How does he feel?"

Sonya picked ineffectually on the delicate petal of a crocheted pillow. "You'd have to ask him."

"You went to dinner at his house tonight. How'd it go?"

"I left early."

"Before dinner?"

Sonya nodded.

"Why?"

"I just couldn't take it anymore."

"What happened?"

"Nothing, really. Just—"

"What was his sister like?" Hildie prompted when Sonya didn't continue.

"She's very beautiful."

"I expected that. The family has good genes."

"She's also very direct."

"She said something to you?"

Sonya stood up, turning away from the window.

"What did she say?" Hildie demanded.

"She thinks Christian is in love with me."

"And that's bad?"

"It could be."

"Oh, Sonya," Hildie was shaking her head. "You've got to relax...let things happen. In what possible way could that be bad?"

"We're too different."

Hildie grinned. "That's the way it's supposed to be."

Sonya continued as if her sister hadn't spoken, "Different backgrounds, different ways of looking at things, different financial levels. And he's not going to stay in one place."

"You like to travel."

Sonya ran a hand through her hair, disturbing it even more. "I don't mean that! I mean he won't be satisfied with me for very long."

"Why not?"

"Because— Because— He can have anyone he wants! Why would he want just me?"

"If he loves you, he must think you're special. I know I do."

Tears again formed in Sonya's eyes. "But you're my sister," she whispered tightly, echoing Hildie's usual excuse.

Hildie recognized the irony and sadly shook her head. She held out her arms. "We're a pair, aren't we?" she asked as Sonya returned to the window seat and her comfort.

CHRISTIAN AWAKENED EARLY the next morning even though he had stayed up most of the night trying to work out what he should do. He had decided to give his quest one last try. He was so close! But he would do it only if he could be sure that Sonya would be safe.

He didn't want to involve her in any more danger, which meant that he only had a small window of activity. He would have to act early before she knew what he was doing, or she would insist upon coming with him.

He made several quick calls. After the last, he grabbed his jacket and hurried out of the house.

THE MORNING WAS ONE of those crystal-clear days that make San Francisco famous. Flowers bloomed in planter boxes and in stands, the sidewalks had been washed by the rain, in the business district clusters of skyscrapers rose into a vivid blue sky, and the view across the bay was perfect. Everything was brighter, cleaner, fresher. The city was like an old tart turned out in brand-new clothes.

Christian was caught in traffic on the Bay Bridge and held up again on the freeway near Berkeley. Still, he managed to arrive with minutes to spare.

The house that sheltered his target was packed tightly among others on the far side of a hill. Instead of the traditional Victorian, these homes were modern in appearance, but softened by an abundance of bushes and trees.

Christian rapped the doorknocker and soon a man appeared. He was dressed in a traditional English tweed suit, ready to go out. His thinning white hair, which fell limply to his shoulders, had been brushed carefully into place and his remaining toilette was impeccable.

"Professor James?" Christian asked.

The old man nodded.

200 *Nightshade*

"I spoke with you earlier...my name is Christian Townsend."

The old man frowned. "Yes, but you're not one of my students, are you? I don't remember..."

"No, sir. May I come in?"

"I'm due at my first class in forty-five minutes. Can we make this fairly quick?"

"I hope so, sir."

The door opened onto an expanse of glossy wood flooring over which several Persian carpets were spread. A series of tall windows formed the far wall, and even from the center of the room, the view of the city across the bay was spectacular. The place of honor in the room was claimed by a black baby grand.

The professor indicated a chair and took one himself. "Now, in what way may I be of assistance?"

Christian waited until they were both settled. "I was wondering if my name might be familiar to you."

Again the professor frowned. "No...not that I— Is there a reason that it should be?"

"My last name, actually. Townsend."

"No—"

"Once, many years ago, you and my great-uncle were colleagues. My Uncle Dominic?"

The man clung to an aura of calm, but Christian could see that it was fast deserting him. "I—I've had many colleagues over the years."

"You do remember my Uncle Dominic, though."

The professor began to tug on an earlobe, giving away his growing tension. "I may. Yes. Yes, of course. I worked with him in Italy...fifty, fifty-five years ago." He tried to laugh. "That's quite a long time, young man. Quite a long time. I know you'll forgive me for forgetting."

Christian remained unmoved by the older man's agitation. "Yesterday I spoke with another friend of yours, Henry Chan."

The professor became very still. "I didn't know he was still alive."

"He's very ill." Christian continued softly, "I asked him about a notation I found in a local news reporter's notes—a man named Ralph Richards. Surely you remember Mr. Richards. He talked with you several times, I believe, shortly after the disappearance of my uncle's exhibit from the Wortham Museum. Does that refresh your memory?"

The man was obviously trying to hide something. Christian sensed that he was closer to finding the truth now than he ever had been.

The old man stood up. "So many years...why now?" he murmured at last.

Christian looked at him. He could see the slump of age in the shoulders, the slight thickening of a naturally thin trunk.

Then the old man turned, anger in his once bleary eyes. "Why *now*?" he demanded.

"Is it ever too late to right a wrong?"

Christian might have hit the man hard in the stomach with his fist instead of pelting him with words, so devastated did the older man's face become. The professor reached blindly for his chair, his breathing shallow, his gaze fixed inward.

Christian wondered if he should have taken more time, led up to it more easily, cushioned it more. But

the simple fact was that he was running out of time.
Someone was trying to harm both Sonya and him, and
he couldn't let the situation continue. If this man was
involved, it had to be revealed.

"What—what is it you wish to know?" Anson
James asked weakly.

Christian erased the harsher edge from his tone.
"Henry Chan told me that you once worked at the
museum. Is that so?"

"Yes."

"What was your affiliation?"

"I was curator of Asian art. I worked there for a
few years before switching to teaching."

"And at some time before that, you worked with
my uncle in Italy?"

"Yes."

"As an assistant?"

"Yes."

"Why didn't you want to see my uncle when he
came to the museum? Henry Chan said that you hid
from him."

Anson James looked away. "We'd had a disagree-
ment."

"Concerning something serious?"

"Yes."

"What happened?"

"I felt that he had cheated me."

Christian frowned. "In what way?"

"He didn't give me credit when he discovered the
Treasure of Tivoli. I had worked very hard there and
he ignored me."

"That doesn't sound like my uncle. He was always scrupulously honest."

The professor rubbed a tremulous hand over his mouth. "I'm thirsty. Do you mind?"

"Not at all. Would you like me to get it? Do you want water?"

"Yes. The kitchen is through that door. The bottled water in the refrigerator, please. In a glass with one ice cube."

Christian found his way into the kitchen, searched out a glass and an ice cube and filled the glass with mineral water. He half expected the old man to be gone when he returned to the living room, but he wasn't. He was still sitting in exactly the same position as Christian had left him.

"Thank you," he said as he accepted the glass.

Christian gave a fleeting smile and sat down.

The old man drank the water then proceeded to talk without having to be prompted. "I've hidden the truth for so many years—from the people who should know, even from myself. It's very easy to convince yourself that you've done nothing wrong. It becomes like a dream. Did I do it? Did I not? A distant fuzziness takes over. I suppose it's your soul trying to protect itself. Like a scar—the injury is still there, but it is covered over.

"Then a time comes, a time like today, when that scar is ripped open and the putrefaction that has been lying dormant for years is expelled. It hurts! But it will feel so much better when it heals again, because this time it truly *will* heal. The infection is no longer there, in the back of your consciousness, waiting..."

Christian waited for him to continue. When he didn't, he said, "What are you trying to say, professor?"

The old man looked at him in agony. "I tell you this because someone should know, and it is no more than right, since you are Dominic's relation, it be told to you. I stole the exhibit. I don't know why I did it. I was angry. I wanted revenge.

"I meant to give it back, let it be found, a short time after Dominic left. But everything got so badly out of hand. That poor man was blamed, the press were like wild dogs, with the police little better. If I had been discovered, I would have lost my job...everything. So I waited, and the man was released. But I still couldn't give it back. I was afraid! So I did the next best thing, I hid it in the museum." He pointed across the room. "Look in the desk. In the top middle drawer."

Christian did as he requested.

"That long envelope. Bring it to me."

Again, Christian followed his request.

The professor slit open the envelope with trembling fingers. "This is a copy of my will. In it are directions to the collection, as well as my confession. If I were a brave man, I would have done this long before, but I am not a brave man.

"My job at the university means everything to me. I enjoy having my students' respect. However—" he pushed the papers toward Christian "—take them. The collection is yours."

Christian accepted the papers. Should he tell the man that the collection already had been found? He opened the sheets and read the first page, which expressed everything and more of what he had just been told.

Slowly he refolded the papers and handed them back. "Here. You keep them. All I wanted was an explanation."

The professor met his gaze. "I am very ashamed. Some years ago I realized that your uncle hadn't cheated me. I had taken an extended holiday. He and the rest of the team had done the real work. Henry and I were off playing, like young Romeos."

"I'm sure it was just an oversight."

"Possibly." The man still would not concede everything.

Christian stood up. "No one else need know of this."

The old man rose as well, shaking his head. "No, it must be told, at least to some. By me, by you. As you said, the wrong must be made right."

"But what about your position?"

He smiled tentatively. "I will test my tenure."

"There is one thing," Christian said. "If we could keep this out of the media . . ."

"I deserve whatever scorn I receive."

"I was thinking of the museum. The publicity would hurt them in the extreme."

The professor nodded. "Yes, yes . . . I can see that. I, too, have been reading the papers."

Christian suddenly frowned. "Professor—"

The man looked at him.

"Have you . . . ? No, I'm sure not."

"You have another question?"

"Someone has been trying to stop me from finding the truth. My assistant and I have been threatened with physical harm more than once."

The professor was immediately concerned. "I would never do such a thing! Violence is an anathema to me."

Anson James was telling the truth. Essentially he was an honest man, caught in the tail of a comet. A lie once told, an object once taken...

A WORRIED FROWN marked Christian's expression as he stepped away from the house. One question was solved, but another remained very clearly unanswered. If the professor hadn't threatened them, who had? Was there another connection of which they had no idea? But who? And why? And could Sonya unknowingly be in danger because of her ignorance?

Christian jogged to his car and drove to the nearest phone booth. Possibly the detective he had hired could be of help in this situation.

He dialed the number on the detective's business card and once he was put through, listened to what the man had to say. Then, galvanized into action, he hastily pushed the receiver toward its cradle before breaking into a desperate run.

In the booth, the handset swung freely at the length of its cord.

SONYA PACED IN HER small office. Christian should have called by now. He would have on each of the other days when they were trying to track down a lead. Was he not calling today because of the way she had acted last night, or was it because of the latest threat? He had said he didn't want her to continue the search with him. Did this delay mean that he was proceeding on his own?

Barbara looked in, smiled tentatively and left, which was just as well. Sonya didn't think she would be able to concentrate properly until she knew where Christian was. He could be in danger and he wasn't the sort to back away. He would face it and laugh. He wasn't indestructible, but did he know that?

The phone rang at her elbow and she jumped. A sultry voice asked for her by name.

"Sonya, this is Letitia. Christian's sister. Now, don't hang up, please! I want to apologize. I shouldn't have said what I did last night. I was just being bitchy. I have my reasons, but that's not an excuse. I'm going back to London this morning and I didn't want to leave things as they were. Not when it's all my fault.

"Christian doesn't know I'm doing this or he'd flay me alive. But . . ." A pause. "I want him to be happy and I couldn't live with myself if I thought—

"I realize I don't know you very well. But if you can turn Chris on his head and keep him there, you must be quite something.

"What I'm asking is, please, don't let anything I said last night influence you negatively. There's no curse on the family name. That's just something I made up as an excuse. I'm good at that. If I screw up, I look for someone—or something—else to blame.

"Chris is special. He does so many things to help people, yet you'd never get a word out of him about it. And he's not the least bit conceited. I hate conceited men. I'm prejudiced, I know. But I do know him better than most. If you're at all in doubt about him, take my word."

She paused for a breath, waited, and when Sonya made no reply, started off again. "My plane is leaving in fifteen minutes. Promise me you'll think about what I said. Please?"

Sonya gripped the phone. "All right," she agreed.

Letitia laughed gaily. "Now if I can only see to my life as properly as I've seen to Chris's. Wish me luck, Sonya, I'm going to need it."

Sonya had no idea what the woman was talking about, but she did wish her luck. Luck was a blessing sorely needed by everyone.

SONYA'S OFFICE LINE WAS BUSY, so was the museum's. Finally, when the switchboard answered, Christian was put on hold. What seemed minutes later, he tried Sonya again. Still busy.

Murmuring a curse beneath his breath, Christian jumped back into his car. If only he had thought to call earlier, possibly then he would have gotten through to her. Then again, if he had plunged into the rush-hour traffic straight away, he would already be much farther ahead. As it was...

He tooted his horn at an especially dense driver. The man looked back at him in bovine surprise.

DAVID SLIPPED SOUNDLESSLY into Sonya's office causing her to jump when she noticed him standing inside the door.

"Oh!" she breathed. "You!"

David's smile was fleeting.

Sonya sank into her chair. "I'm glad to see a friendly face. You wouldn't believe what's been happening. David, someone is really upset about all of this. And now I'm afraid Christian is out there on his own, getting into who knows what—"

"He's a stubborn person." David closed the door. "You have to expect that."

"I wish he'd call."

"I don't."

Sonya knew that one day she would have to face the fact of David's jealousy, but now wasn't the time. She changed the subject. "At least some of the newness is wearing off the latest rumor. I didn't see any reporters when I came in, except Millicent. And I don't expect her ever to leave. Ted might as well hire her, have her do our public relations. You know, like the police turn to crooks who rob convenience stores as experts on how to protect them, underlining the theory that it takes one to know one, I suppose."

David leaned against her desk in the fashion Christian used. For some reason, the illusion disturbed Sonya, made her uncomfortable.

When she looked up at the curator, she was even more disturbed by the expression in his eyes. Normally gentle, humorous, self-effacing—at the moment, those qualities seemed sorely lacking in David.

Sonya leaned forward, concerned. "David, is something wrong? Do you need my help?"

David laughed shortly. "I asked and you wouldn't listen."

"You asked me to stop helping Christian, but what was I supposed to do? Ted ordered me to. He made that my job."

"You didn't have to enjoy it."

"I didn't . . ."

"*At least not at first.* Go on, say it."

"Not at first, no. But later I couldn't help getting curious, especially when someone tried so hard to stop us."

"Was that the only reason? Nothing else?"

Sonya didn't know how to answer. David was acting so strangely. "Yes—"

"I don't believe you."

Sonya had had enough. She stood up. "David, I don't want to discuss it anymore. Another time, maybe. But not now."

He didn't budge.

She stared at him. "David. Please."

Still he didn't move.

Sonya touched his arm. He jerked it away.

She started for the door to order him out, but before she had moved two steps he was shouting "No!" and scooting around her to lock it.

Sonya's heart stopped then started a keening knock as a subtle form of fear took hold of her. "David, I want you to leave."

He folded his arms. "Haven't you figured it out yet? You're intelligent."

"I—I don't know what you mean."

"Out there." He indicated the unseen hall with his head. "They're all so stupid. But you. I thought you were different."

"I still don't..."

"It's me, Sonya. Quiet, silly, gullible David. I'm the one you're afraid of."

Sonya shook her head.

He smiled, and the cold calculation behind it chilled Sonya's bones. "Oh, yes. I am! Would you like me to show you how a lion dances?"

Chapter Fourteen

All lanes on the bridge were moving at a snail's pace. Christian's hands worked on the steering wheel. He should have called the police or should have at least tried the museum again . . . left a message.

Feeling tightly caged, he continued to creep forward with the other cars. Then suddenly there was a break in the traffic and everyone around him took off as if in a race.

Christian didn't question the logic, he merely took advantage of it. The Porsche outdistanced the other cars, until they all were forced to stop again.

DAVID, THE LION! "I don't believe you," Sonya murmured, reaching unsteadily for her chair.

"Why not?"

"Because you're my friend."

"You only thought that because I let you. I'm a pretty good actor, huh? How's your boyfriend's knee?"

Sonya's mind scattered. It had to have been him, otherwise how would he have known...? She ran to the door and tried to unlock it.

David jerked her away. "I think not."

Sonya turned pleading eyes. "David, please. This is all so..."

"Silly?"

"Bizarre. I don't understand why you're doing this."

"Because Millicent was tricked into spilling everything to that detective your boyfriend hired. My cover was blown...isn't that the correct terminology?"

Her breath caught. "So you're the one who..."

"Little ole me!"

"But *why*, David? You love your work in the museum. Why would you want to jeopardize it?"

He smiled. "I like my work, but not the place. It can go to hell and never come back again!"

"But I thought..."

"You thought wrong...again. I hate this place. I hate everything it stands for." His smile broadened in reflection. "It was so *easy*. Millicent lapped up everything I told her and no one was the wiser. No one suspected. Not even you."

Sonya moved uneasily. "Why are you telling me this?"

He considered the question. "I'm not really sure."

"Then why not let me go?"

"So you can go off with him? I couldn't believe it when that workman found the collection. It was so wonderful! I thought of telling Millicent right away, but then I realized that would be the end of my work here. I would be traced and I didn't want that. I wasn't ready yet. Millicent got really suspicious, though, and kept pushing me, but I held out. I can be extremely closemouthed when I want to be. Then *he* came.''

"Let me go, David."

"No."

She motioned fruitlessly. "I don't know what good you think this is going to do. If Millicent has told someone about you, everyone will know soon. She won't keep your association a secret any longer than it takes to draw a breath."

"I don't care anymore. I heard something this morning. The board of trustees is calling both Ted and Dr. Hockly before them." He glanced at his watch. "Right about now, as a matter of fact. It's rumored that the board's going to demand their resignations."

Sonya frowned. "Is it them you hate so much? Something personal, something between just you?"

David shook his head.

"Then what is it?"

"I'm going to tell you a story, Sonya. It's about this normal, everyday family. A *good* family. They worked hard, tried to get ahead. But no matter how hard they tried, they couldn't seem to do it. And it wasn't their fault, you understand? They really tried. It was just . . . hard luck. The father was let go from several jobs. Some people said he was too honest. Some people said he worked too hard and that made the others around him look bad.

"Then he found a job that he thought was going to be wonderful. He came home and told his wife and they started to dream.

"Not long after that, something was stolen from the truck he was driving. Something that upset a lot of people. My grandfather didn't know what had happened. He tried to tell anyone who would listen that the crate had been tampered with before it had come into his care. But no one believed him.

"His accent was funny, and the naive way he behaved around the police didn't count in his favor, either. But in the country he had escaped from, the police weren't a citizen's best friend. A uniform was enough to strike terror in any heart.

"They took my grandfather to jail and kept him there. They didn't let him talk to a lawyer for two days. *Two days!* He was in a cell with drunks and criminals. My grandmother was petrified with fear and well she should have been. The same thing was happening in this new country as had happened in the old. There, people disappeared when taken to jail, never to be heard from again. She wasn't sure if she would ever see my grandfather again."

Sonya whispered, "Your grandfather was Tomas Delia."

Instead of acknowledging her words, David went on. "My grandfather almost died. Did you know that? He couldn't believe that no one would listen to him. They asked him questions, but it was as if they already had each and every answer. And if his answers were different, they took their version instead.

"He was never the same after they let him go. The heart seemed to have gone out of him. When people pointed and talked about him, he would turn away. He wanted to die."

"David, I'm sorry."

"And it was the museum's fault. The director at the time was another Ted. He didn't care about the people who worked for him. He just wanted everything to look good. He wanted the *museum* to look good—no matter what the cost."

Someone rattled the doorknob, then a knock soon followed.

David snaked a hand over Sonya's mouth. He called, "Who is it?"

"Barbara. Is Sonya in there? I need to talk to her."

David smiled coldly into Sonya's eyes as he answered, "She's busy. Come back later."

There was a pause, then Barbara went away.

David slowly removed his hand. "Only a precaution," he murmured.

Sonya tossed her head. She had to establish her resentment of his treatment. Instinct told her he would respect that. Surely a part of the David she had known remained inside this angry stranger.

"A precaution against what?" she demanded. "What are you going to do, David? You can't keep me here forever."

"You sound like my grandmother."

"Maybe you should listen to her. Did she tell you to stop all of this . . . before you got hurt?"

"I'm willing to sacrifice myself. Once I find out that Ted and Dr. Hockly are gone, I'll let you go, too. But only after we talk to Millicent. I told her to come here, that there might be something interesting happening this morning. And there will be. I also told her about the Townsend exhibit. There wasn't any reason not to. So between the rumors, the firings and the lost exhibit turning up again, I think the powers-that-be will decide that they've had enough. I want to see this place closed, Sonya. Shuttered up as tight as it shuttered up my grandfather.

"Can you imagine what it was like for my mother? For my aunts and uncles and cousins? The humiliation...the suspicion! People didn't believe that my grandfather wasn't involved. They thought he had just outsmarted the police. I was only a baby then, barely two, but I remember.

"We were trash in other people's eyes. So some of us started to act like trash. I have two cousins in jail, did you know that? One for murder, another for armed robbery. I was in trouble as a kid. But then I decided I would be wasting my time hitting back at anything except the museum itself. I wouldn't *rest* until this place was destroyed."

His fingers curled into her hair. "Oh, don't look so disillusioned. Be happy for me. I'm about to reach my goal."

Sonya's breaths were short. "This is crazy, David. You can't do this!"

His fingers tightened, pulling back. "I'm *not* crazy!"

Her heart was thumping wildly. "That hurts. Please—"

He smiled before shoving her away. The desk stopped her progress. "I told you before that I didn't want to hurt you. And I don't. But when you won't listen—"

Sonya turned around, panting harder. "Let me go, David. I'll talk to someone, see what I can do."

He laughed. "You? You have about as much power as I do. That's what I like about you, Sonya. We're both workers. We both dislike the system."

"I never said..."

"I almost told you once, about six months ago. It was on the tip of my tongue, then someone came in and I wasn't able to. I lost my nerve. But it does take a lot of nerve, you know, doing what I'm doing, bringing down an institution."

The doorknob rattled again and David stiffened.

"Sonya!" This time it was Christian's voice, urgent, with an edge.

Sonya started to call out, but David again prevented her from doing so. She still managed a muffled sound, although it was probably not enough to penetrate the door.

David whispered in her ear. "Do as I say and I won't hurt him." He touched the cold metal of a gun to her cheek then aimed it at the door.

Sonya drew a shocked breath.

"Tell him to go away."

Sonya begged him with her eyes.

"Do it!" David hissed.

"Go—go away, Christian!"

Christian started to beat on the door. "Pewter . . . I know you're in there. Let her go!"

"Christian . . . he has a gun!"

The hammering stopped.

David grabbed Sonya's hair and pulled her back behind the desk.

"The police are on their way, Pewter. They'll be here any minute. Why don't you come out now, before they arrive? It'll go easier on you."

"And why don't you . . ."

Sonya was amazed at the stream of abuse that came from David's lips. She had never heard anything like it in her life.

David was beginning to sweat. His body, close to hers, was radiating heat. Moisture was seeping from the pores of his forehead. He wiped it with the side of his hand that held the gun, but his action was mostly ineffectual.

Sonya tried to straighten. David must have thought she was trying to get away because he jerked her back. She gave a low moan.

For a moment the old David reappeared. She saw concern in his eyes, but as the muted sound of approaching sirens reached the lower-level room, regret was replaced by hardened determination.

Sonya had no idea if Christian was still outside the door. He had said nothing for some time. She hoped that he wasn't. For his safety.

Minutes passed, minutes that seemed like hours.
David was wiping at his forehead again when a strange
metallic voice pulled him upright, alert.

"Mr. Pewter. Lieutenant Riley here. I understand
that you have a problem."

David shifted position, keeping the gun pointed toward the door. "I don't have a problem. Someone else
does."

"I understand you have a young woman with you."
He paused. "Is she the person with the problem?"

David laughed. "You could say that. But I was
thinking of someone else."

"Who exactly?"

"The people who run this museum."

There was a longer pause. "Is there a reason why
you're saying that? You haven't left any little sur-
prises scattered around, have you?"

David laughed shortly. "Do you mean bombs? No.
Not that kind of bomb."

"Good. I'm glad to hear it."

David shifted position but continued to hold on to
Sonya.

The metallic voice came again. "It's Lieutenant
Riley again, Mr. Pewter. I was wondering...it would
be so much easier to deal with things if you were to
come out voluntarily. There's not really anywhere you
can go. I'm sure you've realized that by now, so..."

"We're staying right here! We're not budging!"

"Okay. Okay. If you want to stay for a while longer,
you stay. Just do me a favor, huh, pal? Don't hurt the

lady? That would be a truly stupid mistake. And I don't think you're stupid. Right?''

David wiped at his forehead again.

CHRISTIAN PACED near the entrance to the great exhibit hall. The police had cleared the building, and even though he protested strenuously, he had been forced to leave, as well. He had no idea what was happening now. Neither did the rest of the museum employees who had gathered nearby.

Barbara hurried over to him, distressed. "Am I getting the story straight? David is holding Sonya in her office? But I talked to him there not more than ten minutes ago. I tried the door but couldn't get in. Then David yelled out that Sonya was busy. I never dreamed... Do you know what it's all about?"

Christian shook his head. If he explained the story to anyone, it would be the police, and he would do that the first moment he had a chance.

An officer walked by. Christian broke away from Barbara. Her dark eyes followed him, surprised by his abrupt departure.

The police officer stopped at Christian's swift approach. "I have important information about the man holding the registrar." The registrar. It sounded so formal, so cold.

"What kind of information?" the policeman asked.

"I know why the man's doing it."

Discerning eyes bored into him. "Hold on... no, come with me. I'll take you to Lieutenant Riley."

Christian retraced the steps he had first taken with Sonya, which now seemed years ago. The last hour had aged him unbelievably. The upcoming minutes would age him even more. If ever he had doubted that he loved Sonya, that doubt was now wiped from his mind. The wrenching twist in his gut every time he thought about what might be happening to her brought that fact vividly home. If only there was something he could do...without her being hurt. He felt so helpless in his inability to act.

The officer led him to the hallway outside the corridor fronting Sonya's office. At the moment, several policemen were there, conferring. The officer who had brought Christian introduced him. He soon had each man's full attention.

"David Pewter has a grudge against the museum. I don't know how stable he is, not very from the way he's reacting. But he's been actively working to bring this place down. He has a special connection with the press. A woman named Millicent Walker. Possibly she could give you more information."

David's voice penetrated the hall. "Hey! I want to talk to someone! Can you do that? Can you bring her here?"

The first officer picked up the bullhorn. "I suppose we can. Who is it?"

"Millicent Walker. She's a reporter for the *Observer*. Bring her here and I might think about letting Sonya go."

"Can we count on that?"

"You heard what I said."

Christian murmured, "I'll get her. I saw her outside."

A CROWD WAS STARTING TO GATHER in front of the museum. Television news crews were starting to set up, reporters were talking to anyone who would talk to them. Millicent, though, was off to one side, alone, smoking a cigarette. She ground it underfoot when she saw Christian, accompanied by a policeman, coming her way.

His expression was grim when he came to a stop in front of her.

Immediately she said, "I understand you're the person we have to thank for this." In her book, aggression was always the better part of valor.

His eyes narrowed dangerously.

Unfazed, Millicent continued, "David freaked when I told him your hired man had tricked me. I don't suppose he felt he had reason to hide any longer."

"If anyone should be feeling guilty around here," Christian grated, "it's you. You used him."

"Not any more than he used me. We had a partnership."

"Well, it seems that you still do. He wants to talk to you."

Millicent instantly grabbed her purse from the bench where it had been resting. "Is it true that he's holding Sonya Douglas hostage?" She was almost forced into a run in order to keep up with him.

"Yes."

"Why her?"

"I have no idea."

"And you're what to her? A friend? A lover...what?" When Christian didn't answer she said, "I know your name now. David told me. He also told me to be down here this morning. Do you think he was planning this?"

Instead of answering, Christian's jaw clenched.

SONYA WATCHED DAVID with careful eyes. Every once in a while his body would twitch. His condition had deteriorated. Sometimes when he looked at her, she saw the wildness in his gaze. But he had placed the gun on a bookcase, seemingly tired of having to hold it, and he now paced back and forth in front of her. Sonya was sitting at her desk, her hands, as he had directed, folded on the wooden surface.

She decided to try her own measure of persuasion again. "I really did believe we were friends, David. It makes me sad to think we're not."

He stopped pacing. "I always thought we could be more than friends. But then he came and you changed."

"I didn't change."

"You weren't as nice to me."

"If that's true, I'm sorry. There were things I was worrying about. Hildie, for one. Have I told you that she's trying to decide about going on with her schooling? It's a big decision. I don't know what to advise her."

"Poor Sonya."

She couldn't tell if he was mocking her or not. She decided to trudge on. "She's very talented, but she feels her work is so different. She can't see that that might be a positive thing. I try to tell her, but she won't listen to me. I'm her sister, so I won't tell her the real truth—that's what she seems to think. She simply doesn't have any confidence in herself. That's the root of the problem."

David was staring at the floor.

Sonya continued, "I wish she'd listen to me."

"Mr. Pewter." The metallic voice.

David's head lifted.

"Ms. Walker is here now. I'll put her on the speaker."

After a pause, "David? Millicent, here. How can I help you?"

"TELL HIM WHATEVER he wants to hear," Christian whispered in the reporter's ear. "Because if anything happens to Sonya, I'll hold you personally responsible."

The reporter read the steel behind the man's good looks and she knew that each word he said, he meant. "David?" she called again.

"I want you to do something for me, Millicent. I want you to check something out. I know you'll tell me the truth. The board of trustees are holding a meeting now. I'm expecting that Dr. Hockly and Ted Armstrong are going to be fired. I want to know if that happens."

"All right. Right now, you say?"

"It should be over by now."

"I'll go right away."

"And Millicent . . . I want proof."

The reporter handed the speaker back to the police lieutenant. "What do we do?" she asked softly. "Those meetings are usually held on the third floor. But that area's been cleared, hasn't it?"

The lieutenant nodded.

Christian moved impatiently. "Surely the director didn't leave."

Another policeman spoke up. "I know where he is. I kept them all together. Come on, I'll show you."

"What are we going to use as proof?" Christian asked the assembled group.

"How about the great man himself?" Millicent returned with a sly twinkle.

SONYA GLANCED FURTIVELY at the gun. David was ignoring it, almost as if he had forgotten its existence. Despite all that he had said to her while they waited, he had forgotten her, as well. Occasionally he muttered something to himself, something that made no sense.

She gauged her relative position to the door. Could she make it across the room in time?

She jumped when she discovered that David had silently moved close to her, a hand coming out to touch her hair.

"I don't want to hurt you, Sonya. You know that. But everything's supposed to be fair in love and war. I have to use whatever's at my disposal." He lifted a lock of wheat-colored hair and let it slide through his fingers. "Just like silk. I've always wanted to do that. Touch your hair. Touch you..."

His gaze dropped to her chest.

Sonya couldn't help her instinctive recoil.

His hand reached out to fondle her breast gently. "Has he done this? That boyfriend of yours? I'll bet he has. He doesn't look the type to wait around for long. He'll leave you, Sonya. He'll take what he wants and leave. You're foolish if you think he wants anything permanent.

"I, on the other hand, would take good care of you. I may not look it, but I know my way around women. The David you knew here, that's not the real me. I'd like to show you the real me, Sonya. You might be surprised."

"I like the David I knew before," she said, her voice trembling in spite of her attempt to control it.

"I don't. He was a weakling. He'd do anything, say anything to keep from drawing attention to himself. He'd let people walk all over him. That's not any kind of man to be."

"He was kind." She was talking about him as if the David she knew was dead, when she was looking straight at him. But in truth, he was dead. Sadness dampened her fear. "He was gentle. He liked to laugh."

"But you fell in love with a man who was none of that."

"That's not true!"

"That you're not in love with him? Or that he's not gentle and kind and laughing...?" The descriptions were made with jesting mockery. "Oh, Sonya, you're as clear as glass and I don't think I love you anymore."

It was hard to keep up with his shifting personalities.

His fingers slid through her hair again but this time grabbed hold and pulled back, bringing her head with them. "But I do want to kiss you. I've wanted to do that for a long time, too."

"David..."

He lowered his head and his mouth began to work on hers. She felt nothing but sick revulsion. He worked harder to make her respond, but she remained as cold as ice.

He drew away, anger sparking in his eyes. "More power to him! He can have you! I like a little more warmth in my women."

Sonya wanted to flash her resentment but wisely continued to look at him coolly.

CHRISTIAN WAITED at the command station. No one seemed to be doing anything! And all this time was passing. God only knew what was going on in that room. If he had been on his own, he would have stormed it. Taken the chance. He didn't care if he died, only that Sonya live. But cooler, more experienced heads prevailed, which was why he was still waiting.

A commotion started in the far end of the hall, the opposite direction from Sonya's office. A feminine voice was raised in anger and fear. Looking back, Christian recognized Hildie and murmured something to the lieutenant. The man signaled the guard at the end of the hall to let the young woman through.

Hildie saw Christian and rushed, sobbing, into his arms. "It's true then? I heard it on the radio but I couldn't believe it. Is she all right? Has she been hurt?"

The lieutenant answered before Christian could. "As far as we know she's fine, and we're going to do everything we can to make sure she stays that way. But the two of you are going to have to stay back. I'd prefer you to leave the building, but I suppose that's too much to ask. If you stay, keep out of the way. It might make the difference in saving your sister's life."

Chapter Fifteen

"David?"

Millicent's call came a short time later.

He scrambled for the gun, again pointing it at the door. "I'm here."

"I have that information for you and I have the proof."

"What kind of proof?"

"How about Dr. Hockly? In person."

David grinned at Sonya. Their last exchange had been erased from his mind. "See? Didn't I tell you?" he bragged. A pause, then back to the door, "All right. Talk."

"What you said was true," Millicent said. "They've both been fired. It happened this morning. The board is hopping mad. There might be a few other firings, too, on the upper levels. They're afraid the city is going to crack down."

David was grinning broadly. "I want to talk to Hockly."

Another pause in the hall outside. "I'm here, Pewter."

"How does it feel to be fired, you..." Again a string of profanity. "Now you know what it was like for me. I never did anything to deserve what happened."

Sonya frowned. David had slipped, unnoticed by him, into his grandfather's persona. Had revenge become so real to him that he was having trouble separating the past from the present?

He continued. "You take back what you said! All of it. Or I'll make Sonya pay!"

"I didn't—I apologize. I didn't mean anything bad to happen to you."

"What about jail? What about the time I spent there?"

"I—I apologize for that, too."

"How much do you apologize?"

"I don't know what you mean."

"Are you willing to repay everything you took from me—my family, my self-respect?"

"If—if you feel it's necessary."

"Oh, I feel it's necessary. I feel it's more than necessary."

"But only if you let Sonya go. I won't do anything until you do that."

David looked at Sonya, blinked, then said, "Okay. She's coming out."

He motioned for her to move to the door. As he turned the lock, she said, "Come with me, David. Please? I won't let anyone hurt you."

His smile, for a moment, was real. Then it became lost in his lust for power and revenge. "I don't need your protection. I don't need anyone. I can take perfectly good care of myself."

Sonya turned away. She couldn't look at him any longer.

CHRISTIAN DIDN'T REALIZE he wasn't breathing until the door lock clicked. Hildie started in his arms. Then Sonya appeared and his heart leapt with joy.

Sonya came slowly down the hall, walking as if she were afraid that at any moment David would come racing out of the office and recapture her; and yet, at the same time, afraid to provoke that very happening.

As she neared the little group, Christian broke free and embraced her, pulling her to safety behind the police. Hildie grabbed hold, too, tears rolling down her cheeks.

Even in her relief, Sonya turned to the policeman. "Please don't hurt him. He's—he's not right in his mind. I don't know how long he's been like that, but he's very sick."

"I'll do my best, lady. Jimmy, find these people a room."

The officer who had led Christian to the lieutenant now led them away. He showed them into a room on the main level and closed the door. "Don't open this until I give you the all clear."

"We won't," Hildie promised.

Christian barely acknowledged the policeman's words. Nothing else mattered except the fact that Sonya was free. She was safe...trembling in his arms. He did his best to reassure her.

"Did he hurt you?" he asked, seeing her into a nearby chair. He had done a quick survey and could see no damage, but that didn't mean that there was none.

Sonya shook her head. "No. Not at all."

Hildie fell to her knees by the chair, dropping her head into her sister's lap, her arms wrapping about her waist. "I was so afraid I'd lose you! I couldn't believe it when I heard..."

"Shhh," Sonya soothed, smoothing Hildie's darker hair. "It's all over now. I wasn't hurt."

"All of us were afraid," Christian said. He wished he were in Hildie's position. His arms felt empty now that Sonya was no longer in them. If he ever got the chance to put them around her again, he wasn't sure he would let go.

Her dark gaze met his, conflicting emotions reflected in her eyes. "David—" she said. "David was the one who threatened us. It was him in the car, him in the lion costume. I can't believe that he—"

A knock sounded on the door and the policeman said, "It's all clear. You can come out now."

When Sonya stood up, she wavered slightly and Christian was quick to offer support.

David was being hustled through the main exhibit area when they saw him. His hands were cuffed behind his back, a policeman on each side. His eyes were fixed on some far-off illusion. He looked neither right nor left.

Sonya watched as he passed. Poor David. Poor, sweet, gentle David.

Hildie squeezed her hand.

Lieutenant Riley paused to speak to them. "I'd like to get a statement, please. It would be better now than later."

Christian protested, but Sonya stopped him with a touch. "I'd rather do it now. Get it over with. What—what will happen to him?" she asked the officer.

"Probably end up in the loony bin. But who knows?"

To the lieutenant, David was just another case in a very long day. No blood had been shed, so he didn't rate very highly in the criminal hierarchy of San Francisco.

AFTER SONYA GAVE HER STATEMENT, Christian drove them home. The sisters had to share the passenger seat, so the car was cramped, but that didn't matter to any of them.

Sonya's body had succumbed to a fine trembling by the time the car pulled up in front of their house, reaction having begun to set in.

Mr. O'Dwyer was sitting on his section of their porch and quickly rose when he saw them get out of the car.

"How're you doing, girl?" he greeted. "I heard about you on the news. I couldn't believe it. Now we've got a celebrity right on our very block. Glad you got out okay. Was the man crazy or what?''

Sonya stopped to smile at the curious old man. "He wasn't very stable, Mr. O'Dwyer. And I'm very tired. So if you don't mind . . ."

"Oh, of course not. Of course not. Don't let me keep you. You get whatever rest you need. And if there's anything I can help with, you let me know."

Sonya nodded her thanks.

Christian assisted her into the bathroom once they were in the apartment. Hildie turned on the shower and adjusted the faucet handle until the temperature was perfect. Steam was already starting to billow in the air.

"If you need help, call," her sister said. Then Sonya was left on her own.

At first she didn't move. Finally, dropping her clothes, she stepped into the hot water. The stinging droplets felt like bullets against her skin. Her body was stiff, unyielding, until slowly the water began to work its magic and she moved even deeper under the steady stream.

She had no idea how long she stood there, letting the water flow over the back of her head, breathing in the comforting warmth. But slowly she began to grow warm inside again and with the warmth came tears. Great droplets welled in her eyes and spilled over her cheeks. Her shoulders shook with racking sobs. She couldn't believe the tragedy of David and how afraid she had been of him.

Should she have somehow guessed? Had there been any kind of signal that she had missed? She was probably the closest person to him on the staff. Was there some way that she could have prevented this from happening?

Her tears continued to blend with the cascading water. Then, at last she straightened, dried herself and pulled on the terry robe she always left hanging on the hook behind the door.

This day could become a dream, if she let it. She could see how easily that could happen. Already some of the moments were receding into unreality. Others weren't, though, and it was because of them that she drew a deep breath before opening the door.

Christian was alone in the living room. "Hildie stepped out to buy your favorite brand of tea. It seems there wasn't any and she thought that you'd appreciate a cup."

Sonya nodded.

He watched her cross the room. She smelled of water and soap, her hair darkened by the wetness. The white terry robe did more to accent her figure than disguise it. But he held any instinct except caring firmly at bay. She had been through enough for one day. He would not add more.

At one point Sonya had wondered if she would ever see Christian again. She had been so afraid, both before David came into her office and after. Afraid that Christian would do something rash. Afraid that considering the way David felt about him, he wouldn't hesitate to shoot. She shuddered at the image.

Christian thought she had experienced a chill and held out his arm. "Come on. I'll get you warm."

Sonya sat on the couch next to him. At first she was stiff, then she relaxed and his warmth reached out to envelop her, his arms around her making her feel safe...making her feel— She withdrew her mind from where it was headed.

Still, she couldn't help looking up at him, memorizing the lines of his face—his nose, his mouth, the way his dark hair was brushed naturally into soft curls. She looked away.

Christian continued to gaze at her. There was so much he wanted to say! Instead he said, "I talked with Professor James this morning. Do you remember him? The man Mr. Chan told us about yesterday?"

Sonya nodded.

"I found out he's the one who took the exhibit and he's also the one who hid it. He was jealous about a find my uncle made—didn't feel he was given enough credit. So he wanted to strike back."

Sonya picked at the ends of her tie belt. "David...David is Tomas Delia's grandson. Can you believe that? He never...he never let on at all when we found the objects. He was angry about what had happened to his grandfather and it festered all these years. He was the one passing on all the lies to Millicent. He probably even started most of them. He wanted to see the museum destroyed. Today, he..."

"That's enough," Christian admonished, touching her lips with the tip of his finger. "What you need right now is the hot cup of tea Hildie's bringing." He flashed a smile. "And your bed."

He drew her head to his shoulder. It felt so right there. After a moment she gave a tiny sigh.

When Hildie returned to the apartment, it was to find Christian scooping Sonya into his arms. Her head was lolling unconsciously against his chest.

Christian smiled and asked for directions to her bedroom.

As Sonya lay on top her bed cover, Hildie and Christian stopped to gaze at her.

To Hildie, she looked like a fairy princess, finally safe, finally protected.

To Christian, she looked like the love of his life.

WHEN THE PHONE BEGAN TO RING incessantly, Hildie removed it from its hook. And when the first light of a new day finally dawned and reporters began to converge on their doorstep, Hildie dealt with them, as well, telling them they would have to wait.

Sonya fought her way to groggy awareness, hearing the mix of voices in front of the house, the crush of heavier-than-usual traffic. Then with a groan she turned her face into the pillow.

She didn't want to think about David and what had happened to him, what *would* happen to him. Once she had thought that she could make all that had happened seem like a bad dream, but she couldn't. It was too real.

Her door opened. Sonya rolled over to see Hildie looking inside. Her sister's smile was tentative. "Good morning."

Sonya sat up, raking a hand through her hair. "Is it morning?"

Hildie motioned outside. "There's a mob of reporters out front who want to talk to you. You want me to tell them to go away?"

Sonya's stomach lurched. She didn't want to talk to anyone, much less the press. But if she didn't make herself available, they probably wouldn't go away. "I'll—I'll come down. Let me get dressed."

Hildie didn't leave. Instead, she came farther into the room. "You didn't seem to have any trouble sleeping—at least, not when I looked in."

Sonya shook her head.

"No nightmares?"

"I had my nightmare yesterday while I was awake."

Hildie sat on the bed and looked down at her hands. She said softly, "When I heard that you were being held, I couldn't believe it. Something like that happens to other people, not to us. It didn't seem real. Then I went to the museum and there was a crowd and the police... and they wouldn't let me in. But I broke through. Christian saw me and made them let me stay. He looked... He was nearly as frantic as I was."

"I don't remember going to sleep. Did he...?"

"He brought you to bed. You never even knew you'd been moved. You were exhausted."

Sonya bit her bottom lip. "Has he called this morning?"

"The phone's been off the hook. I had to do that last night. Reporters came by then, too, but I chased them away." She grinned. "Oh, I should tell you. Mr. O'Dwyer is having a ball. He's bringing everyone coffee and donuts and talking to anyone who'll listen. This is making his day."

"At least they'll be in a good mood. I should probably thank him."

"I don't think they'll eat you. They seem like a fairly nice lot, believe it or not. I know, it shocked me, too. Oh, and there's that Millicent person. She says she feels she's owed some special consideration. She'd like a private interview."

Sonya remembered the way the woman had helped win her freedom. She nodded. "I wonder what's happening with David now?"

"To tell you the truth, I don't care."

"He's sick, Hildie."

"I saw on the news this morning that the museum board has given Dr. Hockly and everyone below him a resounding vote of confidence."

"So the firings were a lie."

"Looks like it."

"David will be upset."

"Too bad." She stood up. "I'll make breakfast. An egg? Toast? Then you can face the slathering mob for a few minutes. All they really want is to see you. They can get the story from everyone else involved."

Sonya was bracing herself to step outside when the doorbell rang again and Christian called out, "It's me. Let me in."

Cries of protest rose from the crowd as the door quickly opened and closed.

Christian grinned as he leaned back against it. "Maybe we should sell autographs!" His eyes belied the humor of his words as they flashed over Sonya in concern. She was pale this morning, but looked rested. Leaving her yesterday had been one of the hardest things for him to do.

Sonya motioned to the crowd. "I was just going out to meet them."

"You sure?"

Sonya hesitated then nodded.

Ten minutes felt like forever as she stood before the bright lights and tried to answer as many questions as she could. When she retreated into the house, she was drained. But she had satisfied much of the reporters' curiosity, being careful to defend David as much as she could. To Millicent, she agreed to a private half hour in the afternoon. Millicent didn't appreciate the delay, but agreed when Christian stepped in to ask if she'd prefer nothing.

Hildie continued to leave the phone off the hook to ensure peace and quiet, and whenever a knock came at the door, if it was a reporter instead of a neighbor offering good wishes, either Christian or Hildie would turn down their requests for more questioning and let them know in no uncertain terms that Sonya would not be available at a future time.

As a help, but not for the people involved, a gasoline tank truck overturned on one of the city's freeways. Several people were trapped in surrounding cars and there was an imminent danger of explosion. The media's attention shifted.

As the hours wore on, Christian watched Sonya try to cope. He could see that she was still deeply disturbed. For Hildie's sake she was trying to behave as if all was settling back to normal, but he knew that it was going to take more time. She had been through a bad experience—they all had—and today was still a day out of the ordinary.

To give her something constructive to do, he suggested, "Would you like to go see Mrs. Delia? She must be hurting very badly right now, what with the theft being back in the news again and her grandson—"

Sonya looked stricken. "I hadn't thought— Oh, that poor woman!"

Hildie stood up. "Don't mind about me. I need to find Patricia. I'm sure she's heard what happened and is bursting with curiosity. And she can't get through on the phone. I'm surprised she hasn't come here."

Not one reporter was in sight as Sonya and Christian stepped onto the porch. The drama on the freeway must still be holding them. Sonya gave a small sigh.

Guessing at her feelings, Christian said, "None of this is your fault, you know. You couldn't have done anything to prevent it."

"I know, but every once in a while I wonder if I could have done something different. Maybe I should have seen something in the way David acted. Some tiny hint. Some— But I didn't. I knew that he was jealous of you, but..." She stopped. She hadn't meant to tell him that. She plunged on. "But I've since come to the conclusion that he was more upset because you wanted to trace the disappearance than he was about anything else. That's why he was trying to stop us. If we came too close, we'd discover what he was up to. He hated the museum, Christian. Hated everything about it. He wanted to see it close. It wouldn't matter that we were following a case thirty years old. If we found out what he was doing, we would destroy everything he was trying to set up." She turned to him as she settled in the passenger seat. "Did you know the firings were a lie?"

"Yes."

"Hildie said that you were there the whole time."

"Yes."

Sonya waited for him to continue. When he didn't she became quiet. From the beginning she had fought her feelings for him. She had clung to the excuse of their widely differing backgrounds, his overwhelming personality, her desire to resist change. But yesterday had settled all of that. At least for her. She had no idea what it had done for him. At the moment, he was giving her no clue.

THE DELIA HOUSE had a shuttered look. There was nothing really different about it from the outside, but in the mind's eye it might have been taking a grip on itself in an attempt to prepare for more adversity.

Christian was very gentle with the woman who answered the door. "We're sorry for not calling ahead, Mrs. Delia. But we thought under the circumstances..."

The door was opened, the iron gate swung out. "Yes. Please, come in."

Sonya perched on the edge of a chair, several cats at her feet. Mrs. Delia chose the couch, while Christian remained standing.

"We're so very sorry about David," Sonya began. "Have you seen him? Will the police let you talk with him?"

The old woman shook her head. "Not now. He has been taken to a hospital. He speaks with no one. Only his own mind."

"Is there any way that we can help you?" Christian asked. "You and your family have suffered enough."

Theresa Delia shook her head. "No. There is nothing."

"I'm sure my uncle would have wanted me to do all that I can."

"What fate holds for a person is unknown. My David...my David will have to find his own way. One day, when he is well, he will have learned to look to the future, not the past. He was always so full of hatred.

I tried to change him, but when a person does not want to change, it is no use."

"If there are any medical or legal fees..." Christian handed her a card.

"I will call you," she promised quietly, putting the card away in a pocket. Pride had no place in need.

Sonya leaned forward to cover one of the woman's dry hands. "David was my friend, Mrs. Delia. One day I hope to tell him that he still is."

Moisture came into the old woman's eyes and was quickly echoed in Sonya's.

SONYA'S HEAD WAS BENT as they drove away from the house that had seen so much sorrow over the years.

"What will happen to her?" she asked. "She's old. She won't be able to care for herself for much longer."

"There are ways of watching out for someone even when they don't want it."

Sonya glanced at him. It seemed a hundred years ago when Letitia had said that Christian quietly helped many people. People like Mrs. Delia?

She looked away. Her heart was swelling with her love for him, but she couldn't tell him. Not yet. Not unless...

Christian directed the car along a different route, through narrow streets, along curving hills and lanes, until finally Sonya recognized that they were approaching the twin peaks that overlooked the city. Houses that clung to steep hillsides soon were left behind and only grasses swayed in the gusting breezes.

The viewing area on top was popular with tourists and San Franciscans alike because its height allowed such a beautiful vista of the city and surrounding Bay Area.

Christian stopped the car and both stepped out to stand at the railing that rimmed the overlook. Below them was the heart's flow of the city: office buildings, houses, streets, people, traffic. Beyond, lay the sparkling waters of the bay and the giant blue Pacific.

"Is this how God feels?" Sonya whispered, awed each time she witnessed this sight.

Christian knew exactly what she meant.

Tears again surfaced in her eyes and she felt a keen embarrassment. She didn't know what was the matter with her. She seemed ready to cry every second.

"When—when are you leaving?" she heard herself ask. There. That was the question that had been in the back of her mind since hearing that Christian had solved his mystery. Did it also play a part in her unusual turbulence of spirit?

"I didn't know I was."

Sonya shrugged. "I thought...since you came here to find out what had happened to your uncle's collection and were successful, that you'd be going back to wherever—"

One hand descended on her shoulder, the other turned her face up to his. A gust of wind whipped strands of hair over her mouth. He gently brushed them away. "That was the original idea, yes, but there's been a change of plan."

Sonya's heart quickened at his touch, at the way he was looking at her. "What kind of change?"

"I hadn't thought to fall in love . . . with you."

The simple answer urged a like reply. Instead, she asked, "Are you sure?"

"You want me to cross my heart? I will. See?" He smiled and put action to his words. "Now what about you? Will you do the same?"

Sonya stared up at him, her eyes slowly starting to shine. She began to cross her heart. But she never got the chance to finish because before she had completed the intersecting line, her hand was crushed to his lips and then discarded for a much more satisfying rejoinder.

THE SMOOTHNESS OF SILK caressed Sonya's skin as she moved about the room, examining one interesting object after another. Christian's bedroom could have used the services of a registrar itself, so many artifacts did it house. Urns from China, Indian art, a silk screen from Japan. Accents in red and gold and black.

Christian lay on the bed, watching her, his midnight-blue eyes vivid with his love.

Sonya looked back at him, questioning a long curving tooth she had found hanging on a string at his mirror.

"It's from a lion. My father gave it to me as a remembrance."

"Did he kill it?" she asked curiously.

"No," he grinned. "It died of old age. It was one of his pets. But he said I'd still remember and he was right."

She hung it back in place. "I'm glad it didn't eat you."

"Thanks. Come here."

She continued to keep her distance, his robe intermittently sliding off her shoulder as she moved from spot to spot. Occasionally, she'd look at him and smile.

He folded his arms behind his head and waited, his eyes never leaving her. He had no need to force her to come to him. He knew that she would . . . eventually.

Sonya soon had enough of her teasing. She crawled back on the bed and was welcomed into his arms. His touch was a flame to her system, his kiss a wanted elixir.

Christian couldn't get enough of her. It amazed him that in another life, the spark of *his* life had found such common ground.

Sonya shifted in his arms. She traced the line of his jaw, his nose, his forehead, the curling springiness of his hair.

Then he saw the object that she held in her free hand and elevated her wrist, holding it above them. It was the small glass bottle.

"I asked you before," she said softly. "Is there something special about this object?"

"My uncle told me it once held a poison."

"What kind?"

Christian shrugged.

"So we should be careful with it?"

"I doubt if there's any residue left after all these years."

"The professor who stole it might disagree. And David might, too, when he—"

"The poison they suffered from wasn't spread by any kind of potion. Jealousy for one, revenge for the other. That's not my little bottle's fault."

Sonya rotated her hand, but not to pull it away. She was shifting the bottle, moving it against the light.

Then it happened. Another flash of green.

Abruptly she sat up. "Did you see that?"

"Yes." Christian raised up as well.

She tried to make it happen again. "Oh, come on. Come *on*!"

Christian smiled at her excitement. It was so much like what he had felt as a child. "I doubt if it will happen again," he said.

"Why not?"

"It seems to be very selective."

"But you *did* see it?"

"Yes." He paused. "Have you . . . before?"

Sonya touched the delicate leaf embossed on the bottle's surface. "Once," she admitted. "When I was examining the collection right after we found it. I thought it was my imagination." She looked at him. "You've seen it before, too, haven't you? That's why you always reached for it above the others. You even held it to the light one time! I remember. You did!"

"The last time I saw it, I was a little boy."

"How does it work? How does it do it?"

"It's a special bottle, one that only catches fire for special people at very special times. At least, that's what my uncle thought."

"He saw it, too?"

Christian nodded.

Sonya stroked it lovingly. "I think it's beautiful."

"It's yours."

"I can't take it!"

"In certain cultures, if you admire something, the host must give it to you."

Sonya was shaking her head. "Oh, no. No. I'd feel terrible."

"Then I'll give it to you as a wedding present."

She became very still.

Christian held his breath. It was a far cry from bedding a woman to wedding one. In today's world, a woman might decline.

"Is that a request?" she asked at last.

He nodded.

She twisted to put the bottle on the table at the side of the bed. "One you make under no pressure of obligation?"

He nodded again.

Sonya smiled very slowly. "Then the answer...is yes."

Christian began to laugh, and she laughed with him until the kiss they soon shared became much too important for laughter.

Then suddenly Sonya sat up again. "Millicent!" she cried, starting to look for her watch to check the time.

Christian pulled her back down beside him. "Millicent can wait," he growled. "*I* can't."

THE TINY GLASS BOTTLE, with a leaf so delicate and lifelike captured forever on its surface, suddenly lighted the room with a blaze of green fire. But the couple in the great bed beside it were much too preoccupied to notice.

H A R L E Q U I N

American Romance®

COMING NEXT MONTH

#337 RETURN TO SUMMER by Emma Merritt

Of all The Stanley Hotel's legends, none was more tragic than that of the whirlwind courtship and brief marriage of a famed Irish singer, Caitlin McDonald, and a dashing race car driver, Blaze Callaghan. History professor Kate Norris played Caitlin at The Stanley's musicale each year, only this time she truly stepped back in time. Did Kate imagine it all? Or did the past beckon to her, promising the key to the love that would always be her destiny?

Don't miss the final book in the ROCKY MOUNTAIN MAGIC series.

#338 SPIKE IS MISSING by Elda Minger

Spike, the million dollar spokescat, had taken a powder. Ad exec Gillian Sommers was given the job of finding the fabulous feline before her biggest client got wind of the disaster. Despite Gillian's objections, Spike's trainer Kevin MacClaine was also assigned to the job. Kevin claimed she was an uptight workaholic who didn't know how to have fun—a catalog of faults Gillian hotly denied.

#339 EVERYTHING by Muriel Jensen

When ex-model Marty Hale bought her family's business, Shannon Carlisle thought he'd be glad of her help in running the department store. But Marty needed help of a different kind. With four boys, a dog and a housekeeper who unfortunately wasn't superhuman, Marty's domestic life was chaos. Shannon didn't want to hurt them, but she didn't know how to be a wife and mother. What on earth was she going to do?

#340 RAINBOW'S END by Kay Wilding

When Quint Richards answered the door of Miss Maudie's stately Georgia home and explained that he lived there, Thea Cameron fainted. Weary and flat broke, Thea and her two sons had traveled for weeks, hoping that Thea's favorite relative would take them in. But Aunt Maudie was convalescing from a broken hip and it was Quint who invited Thea to stay awhile. Thea knew that she would have to leave before he discovered the truth: that he, the local district attorney, shared the house, shared his life—with a criminal.

**In April, Harlequin brings you the
world's most popular romance author**

JANET DAILEY

No Quarter Asked

Out of print since 1974!

After the tragic death of her father, Stacy's world is shattered. She needs to get away by herself to sort things out. She leaves behind her boyfriend, Carter Price, who wants to marry her. However, as soon as she arrives at her rented cabin in Texas, Cord Harris, owner of a large ranch, seems determined to get her to leave. When Stacy has a fall and is injured, Cord reluctantly takes her to his own ranch. Unknown to Stacy, Carter's father has written to Cord and asked him to keep an eye on Stacy and try to convince her to return home. After a few weeks there, in spite of Cord's hateful treatment that involves her working as a ranch hand and the return of Lydia, his ex-fiancée, by the time Carter comes to escort her back, Stacy knows that she is in love with Cord and doesn't want to go.

**Watch for *Fiesta San Antonio* in July and
For Bitter or Worse in September.**

JDA-1

You'll flip . . . your pages won't!
Read paperbacks *hands-free* with

Book Mate • I

The perfect "mate" for all your romance paperbacks

Traveling • Vacationing • At Work • In Bed • Studying • Cooking • Eating

Perfect size for all standard paperbacks, this wonderful invention makes reading a pure pleasure! Ingenious design holds paperback books OPEN and FLAT so even wind can't ruffle pages — leaves your hands free to do other things. Reinforced, wipe-clean vinyl-covered holder flexes to let you turn pages without undoing the strap . . . supports paperbacks so well, they have the strength of hardcovers!

Pages turn WITHOUT opening the strap

SEE-THROUGH STRAP

Reinforced back stays flat

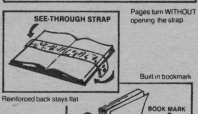

Built in bookmark

BOOK MARK

BACK COVER HOLDING STRIP

10 x 7¼ opened
Snaps closed for easy carrying, too

Available now. Send your name, address, and zip code, along with a check or money order for just $5.95 + .75¢ for postage & handling (for a total of $6.70) payable to Reader Service to:

Reader Service
Bookmate Offer
901 Fuhrmann Blvd.
P.O. Box 1396
Buffalo, N.Y. 14269-1396

Offer not available in Canada
*New York and Iowa residents add appropriate sales tax.

BM-G

H A R L E Q U I N
American Romance®

Live the

Rocky Mountain Magic

Become a part of the magical events at The Stanley Hotel in the Colorado Rockies, and be sure to catch its final act in April 1990 with #337 RETURN TO SUMMER by Emma Merritt.

Three women friends touched by magic find love in a very special way, the way of enchantment. Hayley Austin was gifted with a magic apple that gave her three wishes in BEST WISHES (#329). Nicki Chandler was visited by psychic visions in SIGHT UNSEEN (#333). Now travel into the past with Kate Douglas as she meets her soul mate in RETURN TO SUMMER #337.

ROCKY MOUNTAIN MAGIC—All it takes is an open heart.

If you missed any of Harlequin American Romance Rocky Mountain Magic titles, and would like to order it, send your name, address, and zip or postal code, along with a check or money order for $2.50 plus 75¢ postage and handling, payble to Harlequin Reader Service to:

In the U.S.	In Canada
901 Fuhrmann Blvd.	P.O. Box 609
Box 1325	Fort Erie, Ontario
Buffalo, NY 14269	L2A 5X3

Please specify book title with your order.

RMM3-1

THE STANLEY HOTEL—
A HISTORY

Upon moving to Colorado, F. O. Stanley fell in love with Estes Park, a town nestled in an alpine mountain bowl at 7,500 feet, the Colorado Rockies towering around it.

With an initial investment of $500,000, Stanley designed and began construction of The Stanley Hotel in 1906. Materials and supplies were transported 22 miles by horse teams on roads constructed solely for this purpose. The grand opening took place in 1909 and guests were transported to The Stanley Hotel in steam-powered, 12-passenger "mountain wagons" that were also designed and built by Stanley.

On May 26, 1977, The Stanley Hotel was entered in the National Register of Historic Places and is still considered by many as one of the significant factors contributing to the growth of Colorado as a tourist destination.

We hope you enjoy visiting The Stanley Hotel in our "Rocky Mountain Magic" series in American Romance.

RMH-1